These stories were written during 1975-77 when Emergency was imposed in the country. Rashtriya Sevak Sangh, the organization for which Narendra Modi worked, was banned and Modi had to go underground "to avoid getting trapped by the police and the intelligence authorities, there were many days spent in isolation and living incognito." This experience of the underground movement turned out to be a period of nurturing Narendra Modi's many latent emotions and talents. "I had never even remotely thought of writing anything or becoming an author, but the responsibility thrust on me taught me how to write." Narendra Modi wrote a few stories which were published in Gujarati magazines. Later, on the prodding of friends and well wishers, these Gujarati stories were compiled in a book titled *Premteerth*. The translation of these stories is presented in this volume.

Abode of Love

Narendra Modi

rajpal

Translator
Umang Dholabhai

₹ 165

ISBN : 978-93-5064-238-2

Ist Edition : 2014 © Narendra Modi

English translation © Rajpal & Sons

ABODE OF LOVE (Stories) by Narendra Modi

Printed at G.H. Prints (P) Ltd., Delhi

RAJPAL & SONS

1590, Madarsa Road, Kashmere Gate, Delhi-110006

Phone : 011-23869812, 23865483, Fax : 011-23867791

website : www.rajpalpublishing.com

e-mail : sales@rajpalpublishing.com

Dedicated to

The Divinity Incarnate
All Mothers of the World

Contents

I have something to tell you...

As I step into the world of literature lovers
with this small collection of short stories,
'Abode of Love'
I have something to tell you...

These stories have emerged over the years
Written on separate occasions and
in different surroundings

Whether or not 'Abode of Love' will stand the
scrutiny of being a work of literature
I do not know

But surely 'Abode of Love' does have
the fragance and beauty of relationships
the ring of integrity and truth
Melancholy contrasting with the flavours
of blooming emotions and mirth

The unadulterated endless flow
of a mother's affection
just like the hidden river Saraswati
...the feelings...the intangibles...

This collection of stories is bound
with a common thread of experience
which affirms it

I dare not have the delusion of ranking myself
a litterateur just because my work is
being written or printed

I have not been so fortunate to have an endless
literary flow of words in my being
But befriend words like a seasonal stream
that spouts during the monsoon

I dedicate this humbly
at the lotus feet of Goddess Saraswati.
These scattered words are being compiled
after much loving prodding by friends

Mr. Gunvant Shah has shed light on
the thought processes involved in 'Abode of Love'
He has done this inspite of time constraints
I am grateful to him for this
Pravin Prakashan Pvt. Ltd. and Mr. Gopalbhai
too need to be commended

I had this novel idea to have a critique
written for each story of this collection
I daresay this approach has been
adopted in Gujarati for the first time
My thanks are due to the patriarchs of Gujarati literature
who wrote these critiques

Friends
Neither is this book an abode of love nor
does it claim to be a destination of an abode of love
Abode of love is not a place created by an architect
The abode of love resides in your being
The address of abode of love could be within reach for some
and some fortunate ones may already have reached it
The address of abode of love is in your very conscience
The address of abode of love is all around you
The light of the abode of love is at every
turn in your journey of life
Take a little time out of your busy life
to peek into your own self and I am sure
that you can never fail to discover the abode of love

—Narendra Modi

Introduction

The Sacred Lake of Motherhood

Gunvant Shah*

I strongly suspect that it must be a mother who invented the concept of a "story". It is said that Lord Gautam Buddha was the pioneer of story-telling for commoners. In the preface to Dharmanand Kausambi's *Budhhahcarit* Kakasaheb Kalelkar observes that, "All the characteristics which bloom in a religion or sect could be subtly present in the life of the founder. If this is true, the Buddha surely had the art of recounting stories, skill of discussing its philosophy and an eye for the poetry of all situations."

Universally, the growing popularity of zen and sufi stories reassures us of a bright future for short stories. When "situational poetry" emerges out of a short story, we can see the sculpture of human emotions taking shape. I am hardly qualified to write much about the art of writing short stories. Had it not been for the deluge of affection, I may not have ventured into writing the introduction for this collection of short stories. The central idea of all the stories in *Abode of Love* is a drop from the sacred lake of motherhood. Narendra Modi the story writer had written these stories while he was a young man. That young Narendra Modi hardly has anything to do with the Chief Minister Narendra Modi. The same applies to the reader and the author of the introduction as well. It is not in my nature to critique. I only wish to tell the readers:

---

* A well known Gujarati writer and thinker

"Come, let us enjoy the 'situational poetry' in the eight short stories of this collection. I wish to state from my own experience that the readers' ability to appreciate the subtle emotions in such poetry cannot be overemphasized. It is worth recalling the words of Dhumketu, a giant among Gujarati short story writers who said, 'The creator of a short story wishes to have a witty reader with an ability to absorb. He would always be indebted to such readers.'

What was the period during which these stories germinated in the mind of the young Narendra Modi? On 25th June 1975 Indira Gandhi imposed an Emergency upon the nation. The entire nation was turned into a prison. There was fear and terror all around. The draconian black law of 'MISA' was promulgated. Nationalists in India, the largest democracy of the world, were vigilantly concerned. There were prohibition orders on the Rashtriya Swayamsevak Sangh and 'MISA' warrants were issued on junior members like the young Narendra Modi. It was as if this experience of the underground movement turned out to be a period for nurturing Narendra Modi's many latent emotions and talents. The days of being underground provided Narendra Modi an opportunity to closely observe the happenings and watch the reactions of the people to these situations.

Adventure and secrecy were inextricable parts of this opportunity. Many a times he was forced to disguise himself, "To avoid getting trapped by the police and the intelligence agencies, there were many days spent in isolation and living incognito. However, this turned out to be a blessing in disguise."* To know the outcome of such a blessing let us give an ear to the author himself :

"The reading habit definitely grew as the circumstances I found myself in also made me inclined towards writing. Till then I never did have any opportunity to write. The only writing I had done was on the answer-sheets during school examinations. However, the goal of the underground movement was to awaken the masses and I was made responsible for writing pamphlets and posters for the mission. Writing became a welcome habit. Gradually, I started understanding the power of a sharp pen...While underground, I started editing the weekly *Mukt Vaani* under the pseudonym "Khabardaar". There was a lot of toil and sweat involved in collecting snippets about the happenings around us... My skills of expression, communication and presentation were honed and polished. I had never even remotely thought of writing or becoming an author but this responsibility taught me to write effectively. In the open environment after the Emergency ended, I authored the book *Sangharshma Gujarat* representing this black chapter of history."

A man's true character is tested during times of crisis. The young Narendra was hardly twenty five years old when the Emergency was imposed. The imposition of Emergency became a personal catharsis for Narendra Modi. That is the time he first started writing stories. These stories appeared in magazines such as *Chandani* and *Aaraam*. Possibly some of these stories may score low on "technicalities" but the feelings expressed in all the stories are gratifying. That the young Narendra Modi's sensitive mind continues to assess the tides of the social life is amply demonstrated in *Abode of Love*. Even though the climate of the social life that is expressed through these stories could arguably be more important but the storyteller seems to be more inclined towards the flavours of the holy water of motherhood. If one were asked to describe the character of this collection in three words, the answer would be : Experiencing the Mother. This very experience which encompasses each page of this book, vindicates the title of this book. The author is not a writer par excellence but without a doubt the catharsis is bound to enthrall the readers.

As I said earlier, it is not my calling to critique. I would only like to present few drops of emotions from the lake of motherhood to the readers to declare that a mother's lap is the university of love. There is a crisis looming large over this university in most of the countries of the world nowadays. There are not many women in the western countries who can sit cross legged. Gradually even women in India are losing their capacity to sit cross legged. What's a lap without that unique cross legged posture? Without that symbolic lap of the mother, the abode of love too seems to be dissipating. Actually the abode of love is the abode of warmth, an abode of service and an abode of nourishment. The only event that withstands the onslaught of the uncivilised ways of the world is experiencing the mother. Only motherhood can really face a war. The future of humanity seems to blur without the proliferation of motherhood. I salute young Narendra's *Abode of Love* which is imbued with this understanding. Now without going any further I present before you a few drops of the outpourings that touched me :

- I had brought some flowers to be laid at Mahesh's memorial on the street corner. I was strangely relieved to see that there were no wreaths or flowers for the martyr..for only then could I see through the eyes of my soul - those two glistening drops of tears...probably shed from Mahesh's photograph?

- As Rashmi was about to wipe her tears with a kerchief Rajen held her hand - it was as if the sunshine of the spoken word was about to pierce through the clouds of silence - and said, "Rashmi, such a beautiful drop of dew on your eyes... please do not let it fall... really it's so beautiful... so very beautiful..." But before Rajen could complete the sentence, that hesitant drop had turned into a stream.

- On hesitating for a few moments Rajen started to speak again, "Rabhi... the child has a right to make his mother suffer only once and that is at birth... its own birth. Leaving this moment, he does not have any right to make her suffer."

- It was a quiescent void. However, this quiescence did not smell of the infant drops of rain. There wasn't any reprieve from the gloom while the sun cast its reflection unto the calm lake.

- No... here lies the debris of your father's dreams. I have to introduce you to those dreams.

- What is more important, culture or etiquette? What is more important social norms or club-life? Is wealth more important than contentment? Is religion just a grand temple within the confines of a home or is religion a temple enshrined in your deeds? Does a fleet of fancy cars or a skyscraper define greatness or is greatness defined by great deeds? Does grooming accentuate your looks and personality or is it for shielding your nakedness?

- Jamna stared at Jharna. Looking down demurely, she explained "Both the jowars are to be milled, but the better grains are for making bread for Bhagat and these inferior ones are for me. I will make some bread for myself from these. Bhagat has to work so hard. He needs to have the bread from the better ones. For me anything is okay."

- Amar's parents could not save Amar, but were determined to save Anurag Sir, who had been dying every moment after Amar's death. The wailing Anurag...was today demonstrating a will to live. The consoling words from Amar's parents brought comfort and on Amar's first death anniversary their sympathetic demeanor gave birth to the hope of Anurag's reincarnation.

With the hope that readers will find their own windows of interest, I stop here. Readers are not people who merely read the printed word, often their sensitivities and sensibilities are so sharp that they are able to penetrate beyond the creator's imagination.

A collection of the best short stories of America has been edited by Douglas and Sylvia Angus. This collection of stories is titled *Contemporary American Short Stories* (Fawcett, New York). It is worthwhile to closely read the words written by the editors in their preface : 'These stories present a fascinating psychological record of what may best be termed 'The Age of Crisis', the age in which modern man finds himself teetering on a fine edge of destiny, when his own fateful decisions will take him either to hell or to paradise.' The crisis about which this book speaks of has a deep connection with the pathetic story of the shattered mankind during the world war. The editors note : Mankind saw the barbarism that nations turn to alongwith the spawning serfdom with the help of propaganda by the mass media. Mankind also experienced how self destruction could be inflicted upon by men with the weapon of propaganda'. Actually the history of mankind is in essence a history of the viciously brutal blows upon the sensitivities of men. It is these brutalities from which rose the epics, novels, folk tales and operas. A crushed flower bids adieu only after bestowing its fragrance around it. Struggling sensitivities and sensibilities are nearly always pregnant within the scheme of circumstances. Emotions as these could be considered to be an embodiment of motherhood.

I have a feeling that the words above engage constructively with the stories of *Abode of Love*. The comparison with World War may seem out of place, but it can be said unequivocally that the crisis through which the young Narendra passed left a deep impression on his sensitive mind. To run an underground movement for the well being of a democracy demands courage and patience. The ruling class of those times that imposed the draconian Emergency needs to be thanked for this collection of stories. I would like to go to the extent of saying that the author of this collection of stories, Narendra Modi is himself turning into a 'story' - a story pregnant with the element of suspense. Let us surrender the progress of this story to destiny.

---

* A book edited by Suresh Dalal, *Mara Jeevanno Valaank* (Image Publications Pvt. Ltd., Mumbai - Ahmedabad) included an article by Mr. Narendra Modi, 'The Emergency of 1975-77 was a turning point' (P. 89-91).

The Longing

The Longing

What's a life worth
without a dream?
And...when those dreams are crushed...

A man feels desolate and wrecked. Gopalrai met the same fate in his life. That apocalyptic car accident had crushed all his dreams. The accident claimed Shobha's life and an unconscious Gopalrai lay in hospital battling for his life. When Gopalrai was informed of Shobha's death, he was beyond help and let out a heart-rending scream. His lamentations on that day were enough to shake any braveheart. None around him dared to console the unconsolable. Gopalrai was standing on the rubble of his dreams. The only succour that he could see was in his fifteen year old daughter Avani and his twelve year old son Baiju.

Gopalrai now decided to lead his life with Avani and Baiju as his sole sources of solace. Gopalrai's life was now shaping up to a new routine. Mechanically, he would rush to the bank in the morning, come back in the evening and spend the rest of his time reading. This sort of a dry and unexciting life that Gopalrai lived was more out of helplessness rather than the fact that it was his nature.

Three years had passed since Shobha's death. Avani was on the threshold of youth. She had started going to college where she studied in the first year, alongwith carrying the burden of household responsibility. All this responsibility on Avani's shoulders and the thoughts of what his life would be after Avani got married urged him to think in a new direction. Gopalrai who had firmly decided to remain single after Shobha's death now considered remarriage. It became a hot topic of discussion amongst the relatives. And soon, everything was organized and Sunanda replaced Shobha.

Sunanda could take Shobha's place for Gopalrai but what about Avani and Baiju? The eighteen year old Avani and Sunanda at twenty eight looked more like friends rather than a mother and daughter but destiny had cast its die.

∼

Sunanda hailed from a good family. In the hope that she would find someone she deserved on some foreign land, she had crossed the socially accepted 'marriageable' age. It was quite difficult for her now to get a suitable groom. Her longing to make something of her life before it was too late forced her to accept becoming a wife and a mother at the same time.

It was only natural that Gopalrai would be able to adjust with her, but Avani and Baiju were unforgiving. Avani never opened her heart before her. More than a month had gone by and yet Avani could not get herself to address Sunanda even as Auntie. Avani's conversations with her were limited to a couple of phrases, such as "Here take this" or "Give me this or that". This was heartbreaking for Sunanda but she remained uncomplaining. It was becoming increasingly difficult to carry on being a stepmother. Also, Avani and Baiju were beyond the age of being called kids although they were yet to gain some amount of maturity. While being in this twilight zone within the current state of mind, they were constantly showered upon with the myths about having a stepmother, from the neighbours. All this made a deep impression on their minds which resulted in their disapproval of anything that Sunanda did. Avani, who was used to a life of freedom since Shobha's death felt that Sunanda's presence restricted her and resented the attempted curbs on her freedom.

Sunanda left no stone unturned while offering her affection and warmth to Avani and Baiju. For the newly married Sunanda, her aspirations as a wife faded before her commitment to being a good mother. It was for this reason that she showered boundless love upon the two children. But to the siblings, their stepmother's affections always seemed to be made up. Sunanda prepared the finest delicacies in her kitchen just to win their approval. Both the siblings had them to their stomach's content, though not to their heart's. The happenings on the dining table of that home seemed like that of some restaurant's table for the guests. It was like an assemblage of strangers. She toiled hard to win the children's goodwill to no avail. From ironing their clothes to even polishing their shoes, Sunanda did it all. She took interest in their all-round development, inquiring about what they did at school or college. But, the children took it as an interference.

~

It was Baiju's first birthday since the arrival of Sunanda. Neither Avani nor Baiju had had the pleasure of seeing the melancholy Gopalrai celebrating any of their birthdays since Shobha's death. Leave alone any celebrations, he had not even cared to wish them since. Sunanda decided to celebrate Baiju's birthday.

She started planning and organizing things since four days in advance. She even mentioned about inviting Avani and Baiju's circle of friends. Gopalrai too, thought it fit to arrive early that evening. Baiju's favourite dishes were all spread out on the table. It was time, but none of Avani or Baiju's friends turned up. The four of them made a pretence of eating and quickly slunk away. This was a massive blow for Sunanda and she could hardly hide her pain. This confirmed Gopalrai's suspicions that he had regarding the relationship between Sunanda and the children. That night, Gopalrai gave a piece of his mind to Sunanda who just kept quiet. With all of Sunanda's pursuit towards peace she found that the air in the house getting cloudier each day.

It was two years since Sunanda's marriage. She had not succeeded being an alternative to Shobha, except of course for Gopalrai. This is what pricked her conscience the most. On the other hand, Sunanda's responsibilities were growing. The college going Avani was passing through the spring of her life. She stayed out late after college. It was natural for Sunanda to worry for her sake. These were testing times. All through the day she would be uneasy and concerned, deep in thought, "God forbid if something untoward happens to Avani, would it not be blamed upon this stepmother? Would I not be branded as a negligent mother; Oh no...never! This cannot be. Have I not done enough, that Avani and Baiju can have a mother again? Just for their sake, that I may spend my time for their advancement, I left a good job...and about my motherhood..." just then, her thread of thoughts would get interrupted, and yet again Sunanda used to resolve that she would never lose her purpose, of looking after the development of Baiju and Avani, come whatever may!

One morning, Sunanda curtly instructed in no uncertain terms that Avani should return home after college rather than partying with friends. The simmering discord in Avani's mind since the last two years was out in the open now. She did not have any qualms about being rude to Sunanda and retorted: "I am not a kid anymore that you have to tell me this. I know my responsibilities well...and...and...had my Mother been alive she would never have pestered me and branded me like this." Her temper blazing, she blurted, "Aaw...I know well that you envy us 'coz you are childless." This was indeed the last straw. Sunanda, who till then had withstood all within her heart suddenly felt as if her legs could no longer take her weight. Silent tears rolled down her cheeks. Avani slammed the door shut and walked off!

Avani's words gnawed through Sunanda's heart. She despaired for the simple reason that her sincere struggle since two years was not enough to make people fathom her true intentions.

A woman longs for motherhood. Sunanda was trying her best to bestow upon Avani and Baiju all of the motherhood that she carried inside. She spent the day in contemplation. She was silenced by her own daughter alleging childlessness. Sunanda had never spoken about any of this to Gopalrai. Today she decided she would speak to him. But before that she wrote a note and put it on the dresser in Avani's room.

Avani returned just a few minutes ahead of Gopalrai. The morning fury had still not subsided. She rushed to her room without even a glance at Sunanda. She saw the envelope on her dresser while keeping her stuff back. She tore open the envelope and began reading.

Dear Child,

> *You did not like what happened today.*

> *So many things that I do for you have never been appreciated. Thus, I do not grieve at all about today's happenings.*

> *You were extremely agitated today.*

You reached the nadir when you branded me a childless woman.

It does not matter, it is not your fault.

But it is imperative for me to tell you the truth now. A truth that even your father has no knowledge of.

As a woman yourself, I suppose you might appreciate a woman's longing for motherhood.

I had this longing too. But when I decided to marry your father two years ago. I was overjoyed to see you and Baiju. I was blessed with the good fortune of becoming the mother of two kids like you. Before the wedding, I had made a decision that is not known to your father. Just to see that I could bestow all of the 'mother' in me upon the two of you with my very soul, to spend this life being a mother exclusively for you and Baiju. I had decided not to have a child of my own.

I can only hope that you understand this longing for motherhood in me.

Only yours,
My dear daughter's stepmother,
Sunanda.

As she finished reading the note with a loud wail of, "Maa..!" and with open arms Avani ran towards her mother.

The ifs and buts of "The Longing"

*Dinkar Joshi**

Everyone may not like to read a story but surely everyone loves to listen to a story. It is not that one has a dislike or an aversion for stories, it is only that one is oblivious of the pleasures of a good read, and that is his or her misfortune. But even those who do not like to read, surely like to listen to one.

Why do people like stories? There are mainly two reasons. Either one has not been able to live a life that he desired and being in that microcosm of the story gives him a feeling of stepping into another world that gives him happiness. Secondly, he wishes to repeatedly enjoy some moments that he may have already lived. He wants to ruminate upon those moments which he may rediscover in that story. There is also a third reason - that the story touches upon some hidden fibre of his being which helps those latent emotions to re-emerge.

The most powerful and eternal human emotion is love. Love does not mean just a man-woman relationship. It is an intangible feeling that send the vibrations to create a song in the hearts of men. It may not necessarily be a human, it could be an animal or even a thing. The Venu buffalo belonging to Jumo Bhisti of Dhumketu[1] can never be forgotten even after decades of its birth. The love of Bhaiyadada towards the tree which he planted and reared are unforgettable once you read about it.

'The Longing' is one such tale. The beginning has Ramanlalean[2] standards. While we come across a beginning as 'What's a life without a dream? When the dreams are crushed...' reminds us of Ramanlal

---

* Eminent Gujarati novelist

Vasantlal Desai. As we read further we are reminded of R.V.Desai's story called 'Kharee Maa' [The True Mother]. The father of a teenaged girl and a young boy lost his wife in his middle age. He brought home a twenty eight year old Sunanda as his wife. His eighteen year old daughter Avani and fifteen year old Baiju cannot make themselves accept her. The belief is that a stepmother cannot accept children from her husband's previous marriage. In this case the children who are on the threshold of being adults do not agree with the arrival of their stepmother. The stepmother strives hard to transform herself into their real mother with wholehearted sincerity, but without success. She tries to celebrate her son's birthday to no avail. This too does not go down well with her children. It is obvious that a biological mother would take care of her growing daughter. As a stepmother Sunanda tried her best to emulate the real mother with a thought that people around her should never assume that she does not care as much for the children as their biological mother could have. It was this caring that made her daughter taunt her with bitterness.

The accusations from her young daughter are hard to digest for the young woman married to the widower. She then wrote a note with the blood of her conscience and sensibilities, addressed to her dear daughter. She says, to protect her good fortune of being a mother to children like Avani and Baiju she had kept her husband in the dark of a decision she had taken just before her wedding. Just to ensure that she can exclusively remain their mother.

The concluding words completely transforms her daughter. She cries out "Maa" and runs towards her mother with open arms. Here again we are reminded of R.V.Desai's "Kharee Maa" where the stepson asks, "Mother you are back?" and the mother replies, "Yes, just for your sake."

If evaluated with a critic's eye quoting several academic sounding statements this story could be criticized but as is said about Edgar Alan Poe's works, one can hardly find anything extraordinary between the beginning and the end, but the conclusion always had a punch, a revelation that it becomes impossible for the reader to forget the story. A reason why Edgar Alan Poe's works are considered to be so special. "The Longing" belongs to the genre of Edgar Alan Poe's works. Readable and thought-provoking once read.

On reading this story I had this thought about the author; had he not been a politician, Gujarati literature could have had a prolific storyteller, just as Sarojini Naidu said of Jawaharlal Nehru, that had he not been a politician, we could have got a poet of the highest calibre.

This observation holds true for the author of this story.

---

1. Dhumketu (1892-1965) was the pen name of Gaurishankar Goverdhandas Joshi, a prolific writer, who is considered one of the pioneers of the Gujarati short story. He published twenty-four collections of short stories, as well as thirty-two novels on social and historical subjects, plays and travelogues. His writing is characterized by a dramatic style, romanticism and powerful depiction of human emotions.
2. Refers to Ramanlal Vasantlal Desai who is considered to be one of the most prolific writers in Gujarati Literature and wrote in his own distinctive style.

Dear Daughter Bholu

Dear Daughter Bholu

As soon as the phone was put down, it rang again.
Hello...who...is...this?
Oh!

The editor...?

It was quite clear to Rajen as soon as he heard the name. In the last few months Rajen had received more than a couple of letters and a dozen calls from the editor persuading him to write an article. Today the editor's tone was a little coercing and had a tinge of authority - the reason why Rajen took it seriously while hanging up. He made up his mind to send the article today.

Rajen had never really written anything except the necessary papers during his academic pursuits or a few letters to his friends.

Rajen was considered to be a reputed pediatrician and it was obvious that was the reason the editor was keen to have an article by him.

This young man who had earned such fame in the field of medicine was still a bachelor. Contemplating the various topics he could possibly write on, he went down to the restaurant on the ground floor and came back with a pot of freshly brewed hot tea. As he poured out the first cup of tea, he turned his attention to the article.

What should I write about?

About the diseases that children suffer?

About the high rate and reasons for infant mortality?

About child health and child care?

Their diet?

Of the importance of nursing infants?

No...there are too many magazines which write about these things, these are usual topics related to child health.

Oh yeah...but what then should be written about?

Of the urchins who smoke on street corners?

Of the challenges in the development of overburdened school children who lug five kilo bags on their tender shoulders?

Of the children who grow up unsupervised in the company of their servants?

Or about child labour?

About the parents who travel dangerously with three children on a two-wheeler?

All these ideas were racing through his mind as Rajen finished his second cup of tea.

Turning over these ideas in his mind, Rajen proceeded towards his writing table with a blank sheet of paper and a pen. There was excitement and confusion in his mind. However, the pen did not oblige him with any words.

His eyes were searching for some inspiration when suddenly, he saw the photograph staring at him from the table. It was Arti's photograph.

On the bottom was inscribed : "My dear daughter Bholu."

The letters were written in a beautiful handwriting in multicoloured ink seemingly with a lot of effort.

The thread of thoughts of topics to write about broke and his mind drifted into the past.

Was it not Bholu who had triggered his early ambition to become a pediatrician?

~

Rajen was the youngest in the household. Everyone showered him with affection. Rajen who grew up with this showering of love was full of similar sentiments. Unfortunately he hardly had anyone younger in his own home to give back the stock of emotions that had been kept stored over the years. He satisfied this urge by playing with the kids in his street everyday as soon as he returned from school. It was a routine affair for him. He loved playing with the neighbourhood kids. The adolescent Rajen had this sole desire of being in the company of kids.

During the holidays, Rajen would go to his Mama's home. There too there was no-one younger than Rajen. This time around, the holidays were over and Rajen did not feel like returning home. There were some new tenants at his Mama's place who had arrived only recently. Their ten year old daughter Bholu was the apple of everyone's eye. Rajen too enjoyed spending time in Bholu's company.

Bholu would call out to him "Rajen Uncle...Rajen Uncle" till her throat turned dry. Bholu's parents too enjoyed this spectacle of innocent affection between the two children. The young Bholu teased Rajen by calling him "Uncle". Rajen reciprocated in the same way as her parents, calling her - "hey honey". It became a routine for Bholu to hear a song from her mother at bed time, a story from her father and it was never bed time without affectionate pecks on both the cheeks from Rajen Uncle. Each of these acts had turned into a habit for Bholu.

The vacations ended and Rajen had to leave. Bholu was at the bus station to see him off. Rajen gave a peck on her cheek and Bholu wept copious tears as he boarded the bus.

Until Rajen passed his matriculation, he was a regular visitor at his Mama's. Rajen Uncle and young Bholu were permanent fixtures in the heart of every neighbour.

For the next four years after his matriculation Rajen could not make it to his Mama's home. Rajen's Mama and Bholu's parents would request Rajen to visit them at least occasionally. They too missed him. But his rigorous schedule of study of medicine did not permit him this luxury.

It was only after a long span of four years that Rajen had the occasion of visiting his Mama's home once again. Throughout the journey, his heart soared with excitement at the thought of meeting Bholu again. His boyish frame of four years ago had undergone a transformation in these past few years. Rajen was now a handsome young man with a thick moustache decorating his upper lip. But there was no change in his fondness for children. He knew well that it was going to be an uphill task for him to explain his long absence to Bholu and hoped that the hamper of chocolates and balloons that he was carrying for her would do the trick and pacify her.

He imagined the card games they would play together, of the riddles that he would share with her and of the many new magic tricks that he had up his sleeve. Mama already knew of Rajen's trip, naturally so did Bholu's parents who stayed on the floor above.

Bholu was very happy that Rajen Uncle was coming back after such a long span of time. She was floating in fond anticipation of re-discovering the joys of her childhood. Occasionally she thought of mocking a huff when Rajen arrived, but then she would think, "Not at all...I cannot afford to do that with Rajen Uncle." Bholu was now old enough to think for herself. She was beginning to blossom into a pretty young teenager. Precisely for that reason her parents had started imposing restrictions on whom she could spend time with. Her mother was always hovering around Bholu like a shadow.

Rajen's bus was speeding towards Mama's town. His heart full of fondness for children was impatiently waiting to drown Bholu in billows of guiltless affection. Bholu too was impatiently waiting for Rajen to arrive. She frequently glanced out of the window in anticipation. She thought to herself, "Would Rajen Uncle rush to meet me or would he visit his Mama first?...I don't think so...may be he has his luggage and would have to dump it first." Her mind was filled with so many conjectures. Just then she saw him come. Although she was a big girl, the child in her still remained. She rushed out, announcing his arrival to her mother with a loud yell. She jumped down the stairs, two at a time, and was downstairs in a trice - her thoughts of mocking a huff totally evaporated! Bholu's mother also followed her as fast as her feet could carry her...but her motive in following Bholu was her concern to keep an eye on her adolescent daughter rather than welcoming Rajen.

Bholu flung herself into Rajen's arms. The unshed tears in Bholu's eyes found their way out. Just like it had happened when they were younger, Rajen lightly kissed her forehead. An act that was quite normal while they were still children suddenly transformed into an anomaly in the eyes of Bholu's mother. She was very displeased with public show of affection between them - the lines on her face quickly changing to disapproval.

As soon as Rajen entered his Mama's house, Bholu's mother gestured to call her back home upstairs; and after that she did not return. Rajen became restless sitting there doing nothing. He was bored chatting up with his aunt and Mama. Rajen thought about the reasons that Bholu did not come. Maybe she was cross with him. He went upstairs but he could not see her anywhere around, instead her mother interrupted her own routine to give him company. Rajen's eyes were seeking Bholu who was in the kitchen. He entered the kitchen with Bholu's mother close behind him hoping to speak to her.

Rajen tried to chat with her but all he could elicit was an occasional yes or a no. Such a dry and parched response from her was unbearable for Rajen. He felt that Bholu was a changed personality, in comparison not only to their childhood but even to what she was that morning. It was clear to Rajen that this was an attack on a relationship of pure and guilt free affection. Bholu was being coerced into living a life under distorted norms for the sake of social customs-Rajen was quick to understand.

Rajen could not bear to stand there any longer. He returned to his room with a heavy heart and lay on his bed. He was understandably upset with the smothering social norms thrust upon Bholu while he simply wanted to shower her with his affections that were pure in intention and belief. Bholu may now be Arti, the grown up Bholu for her family, but for Rajen she was still the young Bholu. Rajen well understood that Bholu was repressing her inherent feelings unwillingly now that she was no longer considered to be just a child.

Rajen paced up and down in his closed room. Thoughts racing... his nerves taut... Rajen was tossing and turning. It was so painful for Rajen who still lived on with a kid's heart. Does society not have the power to give sanction to live with a pure heart, with a heart of a child? Why should society look at the age of a person rather than the psychological development. Why does it hammer upon innocent souls-"You are no longer a child...no longer a child...you are grown up now." The very people who encouraged a peck on the cheek of the child Bholu were now raising eyebrows. Why are the barriers of age keeping innocent children like Bholu away from the most pure form of love and affection? Is society not mature enough to understand and allow a soul to live on with it's share of innocent affection? Rajen wanted to be amongst children. When a child grows up to be an adult, it gives rise to a wall that obstructs everything that spells innocence, including love.

Rajen did not accept defeat. He was determined to be with children, so he decided to become a pediatrician. With innocent and young Bholu's thoughts in his mind, he turned back home.

His love for children helped Rajen become a reputed pediatrician.

~

He suddenly heard the knock on his door. With a start Rajen's mind came back into the present. He opened the door to see the editor's messenger asking for the article which he had promised. Disturbed with the recollections of the past, Rajen had been unable to write anything. He scribbled on a piece of paper and handed it over to the messenger.

Dear Editor,

I am unable to write for your Children's Special. I regret the delay in informing you.

Sincerely,
Dr. Rajen

NB : Is it possible to excuse a year from a child's age on account of the Year of the Child?

"Dear Daughter Bholu"–A story of a river squeezed between two banks

*Rajnikumar Pandya**

A normal story is well defined (with a beginning, the core and the end), but defining a tale established as a short story is like grabbing the wind, it can be felt, be filled into the letters, but can never be held with open hands.

The definition of the art of telling nothing directly and yet say everything holds true for the entire realm of literature. Especially for the genre of poetry and to a large extent for the short story. Inspite of that it is not necessary that the short story can take shape. Whether saying something with the help of the power of the word that points out that an idea was worth saying or was it was just a bubble in the air is as important.

A 'short story' can justifiably be described as a literary piece only when it is an inarguable truth, that is eternal, everlasting, pervasive, and has the power of touching the readers' hearts. Whether it has been recounted in a traditional or a contemporary style, in the form of fiction, or as a true story, none of that is important. Each is like a chest, the true worth lies with the treasure inside.

A whole generation of people struggling to be writers were moulded by magazines such as *Chandani*, *Aaram*, and *Navchetan* during the post 1950 era. *Navchetan* has always been partial towards loudness. Its editor patronized the elements of having a goal and a moral, but *Aaram* and *Chandani* drew the authors towards an absolutely neutral and harmonious content, specially so for *Chandani*. I can vouch from

---

* Gujarati novelist and short story writer

my own experience about how stringent their criteria were.

That Mr. Narendra Modi passed the exacting standards of *Chandani* and *Aaram* itself pleads a case for his stories. I read his story 'Dear Daughter Bholu' with that thought in mind. When expectations take root, the weeds of the fear of failing too are not generally far off. These weeds were around me while I read this story - Guards have a habit of keeping a torch and a baton with them. I am happy that the torch was handy but the baton idled.

I have not had the opportunity to read his other stories, but have read my friend Gunvant Shah's introduction. It was evident from it that the central idea of all the stories was motherhood. The theme of motherhood is a cornucopia for literary creativity. Effectively capturing even a single hue from the spray of rainbow shades of motherhood in a tale is enough for the creation of an excellent story.

Narendra Modi's 'Dear Daughter Bholu' depicts two types of motherhoods. One of the avatars of motherhood has a male torso, which obviously is concealed. The remaining of course has a female form which is a little heavy, verbose and fittingly described as a little sharp, a sharpness that sometimes hurts. It is well known that nature has a way of putting such a motherhood into a woman in varied degrees. Sometimes it is expressed forthrightly whereas at some points it seems to be symbolic. There is a clash between the two in the story.

This fact needs some analysis. Because one can obviously wonder how this element of motherhood manifests itself in a male form? A man can only have fatherly emotions in him. Why can't the feelings of Rajen, the main character in this story towards Bholu alias Arti be described as fatherly? Why should they vigorously be classified as motherly feelings?

The physical body cannot answer these questions. Only the heart and the mind can explain. You can get an answer when you see a widower who does not remarry and raises his children without his wife by his side. I have seen many such men around me who are fathers physically and yet, mothers by heart. They could never have reared their children without assimilating some motherhood. The masculine `roughage' would undoubtedly bruise a child. He can only provide the mother-like simplicity and kindness if he acquires the psyche of a mother.

The author's potrayal of Rajen's character is similar. The extreme attachment is not the fruit of his 'father-ness' but is born of the mother-ness of his spirit. Psychologists may confirm my contention. A man is never a man in his entirety. A few elements of effeminacy are always to be found in him. They may emerge conspicuously with the proximity to such subjects. These elements in Rajen are conspicuous while he is with Arti. He may not be conscious of this, for he only recognizes his fondness. He does not feel the need to identify the undercurrent in him. As readers, we are aware of this fact. The thread of compassion for that child that took shape unintentionally, and after a certain period of time, transports him to a point where he starts pining for her. It does not remain limited to the childhood of that tenant's daughter. Rajen has always enjoyed the company of children. He became a pediatrician when he grew up. Even if the storyteller had not described these events explicitly, the superbly developed characters of this story make it self-evident. I personally feel that the pace with which he became a pediatrician in the story make the lines of restraint even darker.

The fact that Rajen remained unmarried is evidence of his devotion to children. Call it the brook of affection or attention which possibly could have been divided had he married. It is indicative of that apprehension which augurs well with the psyche of the character.

The rise of "motherhood" in a man makes this wonderful story unique in comparison to other stories.

On the other hand the alertness or the attitude of protecting a growing daughter in the mind of the real mother displays another type of motherhood. It cannot be said to be inappropriate even after being influenced by our feelings for Rajen but that subtle clash with Rajen surely makes us suffer a little. The greatest tragedies in literature are those which emerge even without the roguery of the characters. Rajen is certainly not the rogue but at the same time Arti's mother too is not the rogue, in fact she is completely justified in her own way. An average Indian mother would act in the same manner after her daughter's puberty and many would say she should too. Perhaps the amount of alertness may vary a little, but being liberal too may not have gone down easily with the readers. This means that we are pained neither by the continual and strict guarding of the mother nor by the acute fondness of Rajen for Bholu since her childhood. In fact it gives rise to sympathy and empathy as well. Then, from where does the pain come which makes this tale a story? It comes from the juxtaposition of the extreme caution of the mother and Rajen's affections. It is not a juxtaposition of the right and the wrong but of the right and the spontaneous and thus the tragedy emerges..not like the seedling but a well grown plant.

In the beginning of the story, the answers to Rajen's "What should I write about?" briefly reminds us of Narendra Modi's lawmaker background. The list of topics which he shows being thought of by Rajen is more like a list of topics that may take shape in the mind of a minister of health rather than a pediatrician. At the time of writing the story it seems as if the dormant health minister in Narendra Modi is providing a background score. To provide a little honest criticism is, to my mind, required in the best interest of the story. Any moral message however slyly introduced, in the body of the story may hurt the artistry contained therein.

The word 'daughter' in the title "Dear Daughter Bholu" is very significant. It underlines the fact that the girl who is crushed and smothered and suffocated between the two types of 'mother-ness' is not a girl but a 'daughter'. We can taste of the nectar in the word 'daughter' as soon as we read it in the title. In my opinion, the title is an inseparable and important part of the story.

Narendrabhai, spare us from thinking that Gujarat has lost a great storyteller so that we may have a good chief minister - and to do that you have to give us even more such stories.

God cannot be everywhere
so He made mother.

—**Edison**

Memorial

Memorial

I had not been home for a year. A job so far away from home, obtained after putting in so much effort, and with a limited allowance of leave, it was beyond my means to do so.

However, today it was different and my heart was longing to go home. Sulabhaben had not replied to the last letter I had written to her. There was a possibility that she was unhappy with me.

While I applied for leave today, it was as if the boss was conducting an inquest.

Is it important?

Someone's wedding?

Mother not okay or something?

Some private matter?

Facing an interview somewhere ?

Bored here?

That was enough...!

There was nothing of this sort, and I gave some vague answer and said it was something important. And finally managed to get three days leave.

How could I tell the boss what lay behind the simple sentence "An important task that has to be attended to." The ruins of an edifice of emotions! In the entire year gone by, I had never been so restless to proceed homeward as I was today, to visit

Mahesh's home. Though it could hardly be called Mahesh's home now...it was Sulabhaben's. The house now had nothing of Mahesh except his memories.

On the third of January, it would be three years since Mahesh died. A stray politician may come across his name in some newspaper or maybe on the memorial erected in a corner of an obscure street and release a word of homage in memory of the martyr. For me though, this was a death anniversary in the true sense. The reason why I was dashing to Ahmedabad in such haste.

As soon as I got back from office, I stuffed a couple of clothes into a small bag and started off.

As the bus picked up speed, it seemed to be dragging me into the past. The time spent with Mahesh during our childhood days played over and over in my mind. Just as a teenager would brood over an unrequited love for an attractive girl, Mahesh always rued the fact that he was not fortunate enough to receive a father's attention and affection. Sulabhaben, his widowed mother, had been sustaining and bearing the household responsibilities with the help of a small nursery school which she managed. Sulabhaben had willingly faced a mountain of difficulties just so that Mahesh may never miss his father.

Sulabhaben pampered Mahesh but yet was mindful of the fact that she should not spoil him and at the same time was careful enough to ensure that Mahesh imbibed her virtues. It were those very virtues and values that attracted me to Mahesh. He was more than a friend to me. His words were ripe and mature and emphasized the importance of his beliefs. They expressed his deep aspirations for fulfilling his dreams.

Mahesh was so idealistic that once a teacher was fearlessly admonished by him, when the teacher had imprudently given an inappropriate illustration while teaching a topic. He never compromised on his beliefs and values which regularly gave rise to many challenges. Of course, it was the fruit of the values that Sulabhaben had imprinted on to his personality but there were times when even she would get frustrated with the idealism that he displayed. There wasn't a single instance one could find where Mahesh did not stand up against a wrong or injustice.

Beholding these traits in her son Sulabhaben would feel a sense of satisfaction. She was happy that the values which she had imparted had blossomed. She was sure that Mahesh's father, up in the heavens, who too had sacrificed his life for his ideals, would be pleased to see their son's life progressing in this manner.

The speeding bus reached the mid-point of the journey and halted near a small eatery by the highway. The sound of clinking crockery jolted me back to the present.

Tomorrow is Mahesh's death anniversary. I will reach his home in the morning itself - I was trying to make a schedule. Every moment, Mahesh's face floated before my eyes. Tomorrow I would offer flowers at his photograph. Why me alone... there would be a queue I suppose. Will I be one of those waiting in the queue or...?

I am sure Mahesh's eyes will be seeking me just as he had sought at the time of his death. And when I offer the flowers, he would make so many inquires with each petal of those flowers. Angry? No... never! My Mahesh can never be angry with me...I was the only soulmate he had. He'll say -

Hey Ankit! am I dead for you too? I know about those politicians who were in such great hurry to get me cremated... so that they may get an opportunity to release their parting words of homage before the press deadlines.

I know of those photographers and the media people - they were in a hurry too! They wanted to print the gory pictures and stories.

There far away was my mother sobbing, but her sobs drowned in the sky-rending cries of 'Long live Mahesh', it was only me who could hear the sobs. It was then that I thought of you Ankit, that you would surely be the only

one who will wipe those tears, comfort those eyes. Did I die for someone's words
of homage, or for a deadline or was it for inspiring someone? Ankit, did I die
just to light up the road for my mother leading to her death? Ankit...Ankit...I died
for the values...the values which...

Undoubtedly Mahesh is going to ask me many questions. Do I have the answers? That I have come here after a whole year just to see your mother who is on her deathbed...

Oh yes, the death was a sacrifice! Gujarat had led a crusade against corruption five years ago. The waves of idealism were crashing against the society's values...with a string of lives being sacrificed. The evening before Mahesh's death, his address was a flood tide of emotions. Every word he spoke shook up the hearts of men. He had been at war to establish the power of the people. He had rebuked the government's actions and denounced the destruction of life and property that was being carried out. The people were loudly applauding each of his utterances. The audiences which stood there to hear him were whispering amongst themselves that till we have such youth among us surely the country's future is bright.

But who had imagined that this dear son of a widowed mother would meet his end like this. On the morning of the third there was news of looting and arson on the street corner. However much he may have tried to accept it Mahesh was uneasy with and loathed any type of violence. He was already at the street corner trying to pacify a mob of arsonists. Suddenly - a screaming siren - and a police van screeched to a halt. And in no time the words of many a political master bore out the harsh truth that "Bullets do not have an address" as a stray police bullet pierced Mahesh's body. They carried the injured Mahesh to the hospital. The doctors there declared that it was impossible that Mahesh could survive. Though blood oozed from the bullet shot, his face was calm and serene, seeming to take strength from the fact that he was dying for the sake of his ideals. He had taken a promise from me, "Take care of mother", and...and... tearfully I had pledged.

I had come...but after one long year to inquire about Sulabhaben! There was a feeling of remorse burning in me. Even in such trying circumstances Sulabhaben had never expected anything out of me. Just once had she pointed out something she wished. It used to disturb her no end whenever she heard the name - 'Mahesh' so she wished that none of the wards in her nursery school carried this name. This was all that she desired.

The next morning I reached Mahesh's home. The scene there was unbelievable. There on the bed lay a wasting body. My mind refused to accept that this was Sulabhaben. Everything in the room was covered with layers of dust. She was straining to touch a photograph of Mahesh lying on a table far away without success.

As soon as she saw me Sulabhaben welcomed me with the same affection. She understood the reason of my visit. "Son, you are the only one for whom Mahesh still lives on..." she said choking on the emotions she had withheld deep within...the subdued hint was clearly pointing towards the politicians who had left a heap of flowers and slogans behind, when Mahesh died.

Sulabhaben was talking about Mahesh to lighten her heart. "Mahesh gave up his life for his ideals...he must be very happy when he saw death staring at him, today though, he must be sorry. The values for which he died have turned into commodities and those very people who swore by them chickened out a long time ago. He may not even have dreamt that he would see this day. I am sure that he would have been sorry for his ideals just remained half baked products of his efforts. Just see...I too am so helpless...?" Sulabhaben's eyes were moist.

Just as I was about to utter a few comforting words to Sulabhaben, a group of youngsters came to her doorstep and called out in a chorus, "C'mon maa..c'mon..its time to vote. Get ready quickly. Don't forget to vote for..." Sulabhaben seemed to get disturbed again. "The same old politicians...they can never get over their obsession with the numbers, be it the votes or..." She sighed and concluded, "the martyrs." She then lamented, "What they can think about is just the numbers that they can get, nothing else matters." Sulabhaben took my waiting hand and held on to it tightly.

I had brought some flowers to be laid at Mahesh's memorial on the street corner. I was strangely relieved to see that there were no wreaths or flowers for the martyr...for only then could I see through the eyes of my soul - those two glistening drops of tears...probably shed from Mahesh's photograph?

Whose 'Memorial' - of the martyr or of ideals and values?

*Hasmukh Rawal**

It has been recorded very often that Mr. Narendra Modi was not the Chief Minister of Gujarat when these stories were written. I am fortunate that I have had the opportunity to read each of these stories before this collection was published. Therefore I wish to emphasise that surely one can see a hint of the future "Gujarat no nath" and "Chhote Sardar". This is because as a Chief Minister today he is still committed to heal the pain of a drought of an emotional nationalism during and even after the emergency. He has opened the flood gates of his emotion filled world and continues to keep pouring his deepest feelings by carrying out many constructive projects for the development of the people of Gujarat.

In this collection, he has accurately given a shape to the roaring ocean of emotions of his heart. The numerous reflections of the inner battles-crusades-struggles of the past (and also the present) have been very effectively depicted.

Speaking about the story "Memorial" - the detachment of an artist or the skill of the author is well defined in the beginning of the story itself. Looking at the title it creates an impression that it may be a folk tale. However, after reading the story it unerringly expresses the universal question that is troubling this era - the entombment of ideals and values.

It is necessary for any author that he does not disclose the central idea of the story in the very beginning. To justify this there is a detailed account of the difficulties that Ankit, Mahesh's friend, faces while he

---

* Well known Gujarati novelist and columnist

struggles hard to get leave from his job. After this restrained introduction, Ankit casually refers to Sulabhaben, the mother and then about the anniversary of Mahesh's martyrdom. Then in a few words he talks about how Mahesh was not fortunate enough to have his father's umbrella of support since childhood. About his mother Sulabhaben who showers him with so much love and affection so that he may not miss his father. All this, inspite of the difficulties she faced while she brought him up along with running a nursery school. Then in a nutshell he describes the truth about how her ideals were transferred into the son's mind. The idealistic woman and a loving mother's image has been very well drawn out. A mother who has sacrificed her life for the sake of moulding her son in the image of her ideals.

The homebound Ankit's thought processes now advance further...

"Why me alone..., there would be a queue I suppose." At that point a vital fact flashes in Ankit's mind.

Further on... "Will I be one of them waiting in the queue or..?"

Not only does this simply point out the rigours of the social, political realities of life but at a micro level it pointedly stresses upon it. At this juncture a sensitive reader understands the root of the concept of Narendrabhai Modi's story.

When a common man is martyred, he lives on forever for his near and dear ones.

What about the leaders, the photographers and the newspaper-men? The leaders who were present at the martyr's funeral were impatient so that they may be able to speak for the benefit of the evening news. The photographers were in a hurry so that they may be able to print the martyr's photographs and their headlines...so that their papers may have a larger circulation. That was the time when the mother was sobbing in the background of the cries of "Long live Mahesh". Was there anyone who could hear those painful sobs?

While the evil of corruption is spreading in the country and the world, Mahesh had given up his life to a police bullet during the anti-corruption movement in Gujarat.

Years had passed and the ailing Sulabhaben lay there on a bed.

The mother tells Ankit :

"Mahesh gave up his life for his ideals... he must be very happy when he saw death staring at him, today though he must be sorry. The values for which he died have turned into commodities and those people who swore by them, chickened out since long."

Narendrabhai Modi then gives a gentle twist -

The group of youngsters who persuade people to vote and then the murmurs of "majority" politics.

It concludes with Ankit and Sulabhaben at the memorial where they do not see a single flower adorning the memorial stone.

Room No. 9

Room No. 9

Rajen was driving the car much against the wishes of everyone in the family. As always he was bubbling with enthusiasm but none in the family shared his exuberance. Everyone including Dad and Rashmi were silent. It was like each one of those riding in the car was covered with a shroud of silence. Rajen though was detached from all of them. His sudden fits of laughter were like streaks of lightning in that dismal air.

As soon as the car halted in the porch of the cancer hospital, Rajen called out "C'mon Dad...we've reached the destination."

These words from Rajen seared each heart. "No...Bro...just an encampment," joked Rashmi in an attempt to lighten the air. However, she could not control the pain which was welling up as tears in her eyes.

As Rashmi was about to wipe her tears with a kerchief Rajen held her hand - it was as if the sunshine of the spoken word was about to pierce through the clouds of silence - and said, "Rashmi, such a beautiful drop of dew on your eyes... please do not let it fall... really it's so beautiful... so very beautiful..." But before Rajen could complete the sentence, that hesitant drop had turned into a stream.

The hospital entrance was adorned with a row of well tended pots of flowering plants. The gardener was busy clearing the debris of dry flowers and leaves from the pots.

Rajen true to his nature never missed an opportunity to make friends.

"Hey, beautiful flowers there!" he shouted out gaily and succeeded in getting the gardener's attention. The gardener gave a hint of a smile and turned back to his flowers.

Rajen tried to push the conversation ahead with words of appreciation, "Wow...you hardly leave any dead flowers back eh...?"

The gardener answered philosophically without lifting his head, "Sir...this garden belongs to a hospital and here we tend life."

Rajen pondered over the gardener's words while climbing the stairs with his father and sister, 'This is a hospital, they tend lives here. Would he be tended to...'

"Rashmi..." he called out breaking the silence, "It would be great if all the doctors became gardeners first!"

Before anyone could answer, the nurse gestured and said, "Room No. 9."

"Thank you very much Sister!" said Rajen in his usual cheery style and entered Room No. 9. "Whew...reached our 'camp' at last." He was careful not to use the word 'destination' this time fearing it may hurt Rashmi's sentiments.

Rajen had been visiting various hospitals, big and small and was now habituated to such visits. He knew the hospital protocols to be followed. His joy lay in living mirthfully, whether surrounded by live people or inanimate things, it did not matter. Rajen counted on this joy which lay in the deep recesses of his heart to take him across the journey of life. He had been living with this small wish ingrained in his heart. Even amid the physical and mental pain all his actions oozed joy.

Eighteen months ago Rajen had been diagnosed with cancer but he had never let that fact reflect in his behaviour. In fact he was livelier than ever before. The term "cancer" upset the family, but Rajen's joyous demeanour injected an element of hope in everyone's lives.

It seemed as if Rajen's mission was - 'Life is death for the one who fears life.' Even death loves the company of such lives.

Room No. 9 resounded with a joyous air which was not to be found elsewhere in the depressing atmosphere of the hospital. It was hardly an hour since Rajen had been admitted in the hospital but everyone who passed by was forced to take note of Room No. 9 and Rajen. The walls of the room were experiencing the sounds of unbridled laughter for the first time since they were built. Till then they had only heard the moans, cries of pain and occasionally sobs from someone's deathbed.

This was indeed the first occasion that they were echoing the sounds of laughter, joy and the notes of cheer. Just like a braveheart who was trying to shower the fragrance of life upon death.

It was easy for the cold walls of the room to echo these sounds of mirth but it was not possible for Dad and Rashmi's faces to reflect anything but pain.

"Rajenbabu..." called the nurse softly as she entered the room handing him a pair of hospital clothes, "These are special clothes... there's a rule that you..."

"Sister, it seems that you have joined recently!" a smiling Rajen initiated a conversation to get acquainted.

"But, how did you know?" said the surprised nurse.

"The way you entered the room, I noticed the excitement and I am sure an old hand would never have this excitement and such flurry in her gait. Just that..." said Rajen appreciating her with an aim to win her attention and simultaneously reminded her of her duty too.

"Thanks..." replied the nurse.

"Hey...Just a dry thank you is not enough. You have a brand new job, that certainly calls for a treat..." Rajen said, cultivating some amount of proximity in the very first encounter itself.

It was the first day at the hospital. And Room No. 9 bustled with activity. A number of doctors came to examine Rajen. The nurse came regularly for recording Rajen's temperature and also gave him a couple of injections. Rajen's long term case history papers were being circulated among various specialists and departments. The new treatment had not yet been initiated as Rajen's observation report was still being prepared.

The seriousness of Rajen's illness was not unknown to the doctors. Since Rajen needed to have complete bed rest, all the hospital staff were given strict orders to the effect by the doctor. It was however hard to restrain Rajen. Inspite of the nurses' tough stance, he succeeded in walking out of the room.

Defying the doctor's orders, Rajen explored the whole floor. He spoke to a lot of people - empathizing with someone's pain and even listening to complaints.

He returned to his room as the sun was about to set. Just then Rashmi was returning from home with something to eat. Rajen thought to himself, "Good that Rashmi reached only after I was back or she..."

In the past, whenever Rajen was hospitalized, it was always Rashmi who acted as the caregiver. Even today Rashmi had come prepared for it but Rajen persuaded her to return home since he was feeling relatively well.

≈

Sounds of the early morning hospital routine woke Rajen from his sleep. The housekeeping staff seemed to have taken over the place completely. Each corner was being cleaned meticulously. Rajen could see from the lobby of his floor that even the gardener was engrossed in his routine. He remembered the gardener's words again, "Here we tend life."

Suddenly Rajen remembered that Dr. Rao, the chief doctor of the hospital would be making a visit today.

Rashmi had still not come. The household routines might have delayed her. How hard she toils! Whenever Rajen was left alone, invariably his compassion for others would surface. He would think of Rashmi and about what she was going through just for his sake. All this repeatedly played over and over in his mind.

"May I come in?" A sweet voice woke him up from the stupor of his thoughts. Rajen tried to get back his calm, but failed to erase the distressing lines of concern emanating from his thoughts.

Before he could answer, a woman about twenty five or so, with striking looks, seemingly from a good family, who had an attractive smile on her face and an imposing personality, where nature had seemingly been very kind in moulding her frame and left no stone unturned in bestowing her with beauty; stood there beside Rajen's bed.

"Rajenbabu, you..." she said with a tinkle in her voice and smiled. Before the woman could finish the sentence Rajen said, "Not Rajenbabu, everyone calls me just Rajen." Again she smiled in a manner that one would want her to keep on smiling.

"Please get well soon" saying this she put a rose in Rajen's hand.

Rajen, who had the skill to impress anyone in the very first meeting was at a loss for words this time.

"Please...sit down" said Rajen hesitatingly, gesturing towards a stool near his bed.

She sat on the stool without hesitation but in a moment stood up "Rajenbabu..."

"Hmm..mm" Rajen nodded his head in the negative.

"Okay...Rajen...some other time" she finshed the sentence and started to walk away.

Rajen could not think of anything at that moment, so he asked, "Your name...?"

"Rabhi..." she beamed and to Rajen it seemed like a beautiful dream.

Rajen was left repeating the word : "Rabhi."

Just then Rashmi entered with tea and breakfast but Rajen was still lost in a daze after his encounter with Rabhi.

Suddenly there was a flurry of activity! It did not take time for Rajen to understand that Dr. Rao had arrived.

Dr. Rao was meeting the patients in every room individually. Senior and junior house doctors and a group of nurses were following him.

As soon as he entered Room No. 9, Rajen stood up and greeted him, "Good morning, Doctor" and welcomed everyone. Hearing the ring of his voice Dr. Rao momentarily thought that it was a patient's relative who might have greeted him.

Dr. Rao began studying the case papers. While going through the details in the papers he was glancing at Rajen off and on. He stared at Rajen a few times and saw the same smiling face of Rajen each time.

Dr. Rao spent considerable time with Rajen. He put many questions to Rajen. Dr. Rao's questions were striving to differentiate the thin line between life and death and inspite of the serious nature of his queries, Rajen's answers were exposing the truth of life - wrapped in laughter and mirth.

Dr. Rao was impressed with Rajen in that short interview but the medical history in the case papers was troubling him.

Before Dr. Rao could step away Rajen said lightly, "Dr. Rao, Sir, I wish to congratulate you!" There was a sparkle in Rajen's eyes.

Dr. Rao paused for a moment and inquired "Why?"

"With your efforts, the arrangements here are very nice. The ambience here is so peaceful and serene that it makes me feel even dying here would be enjoyable."

Dr. Rao who was intently listening to Rajen was startled to hear him say this. Everyone who had come with Dr. Rao looked wonderingly at Rajen.

Dr. Rao couldn't say anything more than, "Oh young man...!"

~

It had been a busy day with different specialists and nurses zipping in and out of Rajen's room. There was an increase in the number of injections and tablets being administered for his treatment.

Rajen had questioned the staff and ferreted out the fact that it was Rabhi's routine every morning to meet each patient in the hospital and hand a fresh rose to each one of them.

Even before the sun was out, Rajen was up and waited eagerly for the arrival of Rabhi and kept looking expectantly at the door.

Rabhi entered the room along with the first rays of the sun from the east.

The formal, "May I come in?" was missing. "Good Morning Rajen!" said Rabhi and stood beside Rajen.

"Rabhi, I had already inquired about you and knew that this morning would kickstart with your visit," said Rajen without reciprocating the greeting.

Rabhi was looking at Rajen with a smile on her face.

"Rabhi, do you realize how your routine illustrates the truth of life to everyone who has come here! Compared to the oxygen cylinders, the injections, the tablets and the medicines, yours is the simplest way that reaffirms the essence of life."

Listening to Rajen's words Rabhi was eager to hear more.

It was for the first time that the halo of Rajen's personality was influencing Rabhi and the co-existing splendour of both was enough to pale the sun rays that peeped through into the room.

Rajen suddenly stopped speaking.

Rabhi could not resist asking "Essence of life and yet simple?"

"Yeah, Rabhi, that is indeed the truth of life."

"But what?" inquired Rabhi a little impatiently.

There was no lack of patience visible on Rajen's face. The calm and comfort which were to be seen on Rabhi's face yesterday were now apparent on the face of Rajen.

"Hey Rabhi, the flower which you gifted yesterday was so lovely and fresh. Today the rose seems stale. This is true for the patients here. The present state of yesterday's rose is the future of today's patient. It arrives here to get stale. The only difference is the delicateness of the hands and the clean bedsheets.

"Oh! yes, and there is another truth connected with it. When the rose blossomed even the thorns were sparing but as soon as it wilted they too become so heartless, rigid, sharp and dry. However, Rabhi, even though I know of this truth, I aspire to rise above it. I know well that just like the rose I too will wilt, and I fear that the people who are concerned for me, who care for me, who insulate me, should not lose their compassion...hoping they may not turn heartless and insensitive. That is the only reason I wish to dedicate compassion, mirth... to them...actually strive to drench them in it!"

Saying all this Rajen seemed to get tired and slumped back on his pillow.

Hearing Rajen's words, Rabhi felt a cold grip tighten over her heart. She failed to realize that Rajen had now stopped talking - his words were still ringing in her ears.

She jolted back from her thoughts as she heard Rajen asking for a glass of water. Rajen extended his hand to take the glass of water which she held out in her hand. "That's fine...Thank you!" Rajen replied without a hint of a smile.

All of a sudden Rajen remembered that he had not offered

a seat to Rabhi and offered her the bedside stool with a gesture.

"Some other time in leisure...today I am in a hurry," said Rabhi but deep inside she could not miss the feeling of a yearning to sit there and have a long chat.

As she turned to leave Rajen's side, she stared long and hard at him. Her legs were carrying her towards the door but her mind was still not ready to go.

As Rabhi was stepping out, Rajen asked her with a smile on his face, "So Rabhi, seems you did not like the stuff I said, right?"

"Oh no, not at all..nothing of the sort" Rabhi was at a loss for words.

"Then what about the rose today..."

Rabhi had avoided giving the rose but Rajen himself claimed it.

It seemed that Rabhi was was not as keen as yesterday to give the flower. "Rabhi, even if you do not offer me the flower, the truth may be ignored, but never can it be concealed."

Rabhi turned back and handed the rose to him.

"Rabhi, this smiling rose reminds me of..."

And Rabhi was gone, wearing just a hint of a smile.

Rajen's words occupied Rabhi's mind for the whole day.

Rabhi could not control the urge of going again to meet Rajen. There she stood before Rajen again, in the evening.

~

Rajen had been feeling unwell throughout the day. He was breathing heavily, frequently coughing and was feeling weak too. For the first time while cleaning the sputum cup Rashmi noticed that Rajen was losing blood through the sputum.

After the hard work that the doctors had put in through the day Rajen was a little relieved. Rashmi had adjusted the backrest of his bed at an angle of 45 degrees. At that moment it did not seem that Rajen's body had gone through such intolerable pain through the day.

Rajen welcomed Rabhi with a smile as soon as she entered. Rabhi could guess Rajen's condition seeing him sitting with the help of the backrest.

"Rabhi..." Rajen started in a light tone.

"Good that you've come again, Rabhi." Rajen was a little emotional. "One who has sacrificed everything to care for this body of mine, and showers such care when the result is preordained. One who has such aspirations for this body, who has taken upon these responsibilities at such a young age..."

Rajen started coughing as he was speaking. After a brief spell of rest he started again, "One who has never deprived me of anything that I may wish for...my darling kid sister Rashmi..."

Rabhi was absorbing the description of such a life with awe. There was revered respect for Rashmi in her silence.

"Rajen..." Rabhi said breaking the silence "You are fortunate to have such a sister."

"Nature is so strange, a brother like me for a sister like Rashmi, but diseased and dying...so unfortunate!"

Before Rajen could speak any further, Rashmi silently put her hand on Rajen's mouth requesting him to stop.

"Rabhi, if I have an opportunity to paint a picture combining labour, the spirit of surrender and faith it would definitely look like Rashmi..."

Rabhi sensed that Rashmi was getting uncomfortable hearing her praise, so she tried to change the topic.

"Oh! So you are a painter?" her question concealed a feeling of appreciation.

"Not really, have painted just one portrait of my Mother, after her death"

Rajen could not say anything more as his eyes moved from

Rabhi to Rashmi and back.

"I am sorry Rajen, very sorry. I shouldn't have broached this topic," said Rabhi apologetically looking at a dejected Rajen realizing that she had touched upon something inappropriate.

"Not at all Rabhi, there is no reason for you to be apologetic. The joy of living cannot be obtained by separating the truth from life. Perhaps it is just that the illusion of enjoying one's life is maintained by doing that. She was an epitome of love. When Mother was dying I hated her having to die, it was unbearable for me. However, today I feel what happened was for good...that Mother departed earlier..." he was speaking calmly and his eyes were steady.

Neither Rabhi nor Rashmi could really get a grip on what Rajen wanted to express. They were only empathizing with him.

"Yes... the incident was unbearable. She was an epitome of love. A great loss... and inspite of recollecting all of this I still feel that God's decision that she is no longer alive was indeed appropriate."

After a pause he started to speak again, "Rabhi... a child has a right to make his mother suffer only once and that is at birth...its own birth. Other than that moment, he does not have any right to make her suffer."

"But Rabhi...had Mother been alive today... she would have been very unhappy looking at the condition of her child. She could never have accepted my death. And I would have been an instrument for her sorrow. God, however understands." saying this, Rajen fell back on his pillow.

"Rajen... brother... you will get tired. Please rest," Rashmi requested him to to rest.

As Rajen drifted off into sleep, Rabhi and Rashmi started chatting. As Rashmi learnt about how Rabhi had involved herself in this work and for people who were total strangers to her, she felt a great sense of respect for Rabhi. Though Rajen was the central topic of their conversation Rashmi occasionally inquired about Rabhi's life too.

Rabhi was completely involved in doing social service. Her life's joy lay in working for the well being of others. She did not have any personal ambitions, happiness, aspirations, expectations, nothing at all. She had decided to remain single for the sake of serving others - Rashmi could glean many such things from the conversation with Rabhi.

Engrossed in their conversation they did not realize that the sun had set. Rabhi stood up to go home and suggested that she could drop Rashmi home. But Rashmi planned to stay in the hospital, though much against Rajen's wish.

"Today Rajen has to remain without water throughout the night. Dr. Rao will be coming tomorrow for some tests with the fiber optic gastroscope," citing the reason for her staying.

Reaching home Rabhi decided that the next morning she would rise early and go to the hospital.

Throughout the night Rajen was restless and woke Rashmi up several times to adjust the backrest so that he could get some sleep. Rashmi too kept awake to provide company to Rajen. Unable to sleep both of them chatted into the night. Rashmi told Rajen many things that Rabhi had shared with Rashmi - especially regarding her personal life.

Inspite of having a sleepless night Rajen was up early and refreshed himself. Rabhi too arrived earlier than she normally did. She had the same smile as she had at the first meeting with Rajen. He had a look on his face which clearly showed the awe with which he perceived Rabhi.

Dr. Rao visited Rajen's room before proceeding to the operation theatre. His visit was unexpected, but Rajen welcomed him as usual.

Though Rajen had happiness written on his face, Dr. Rao

seemed dejected. As he checked all the case papers and reports of Rajen again, Dr. Rao seemed deep in thought.

The ward boys had come to take Rajen away on a stretcher. Seeing the stretcher, Rajen looked amused and laughed loudly which drew everyone's attention. Rajen did not want to be taken on a stretcher, he would much rather walk.

But in Dr. Rao's opinion Rajen should be moved to the operation theatre only on a stretcher.

"Rajen, looking at the condition of your health, you need to take complete rest, walking like this..." Dr. Rao expressed his concern.

Finally, agreeing with Dr. Rao, Rajen moved on to the stretcher. Rajen played with a rose as he was being moved to the operation theatre. Rashmi and Rabhi were escorting him.

"Dr. Rao...Sir, I am aware that you care for me more than just a doctor as nothing from my past or the present is unknown to you. Doctor, I am also aware that the cannonball appearance you came across in my bone X-rays and chest X-rays have worried you and the liver function tests as well. I do know that my last report shows that I suffer from secondary lung cancer. I know well that you are striving to find the source of the cancer. During your investigations you have also come across an ulcer on the greater curvature of the stomach. Today you are to determine whether it is just an ulcer or a sarcoma."

Rajen was speaking in a steady mechanical monotone, as if he was detached from his body.

Dr. Rao was fully aware of the truth that Rajen was speaking about. He was just so taken aback at the way Rajen had prepared his mind to bear the consequences and that was what was attracting Dr. Rao towards Rajen.

Rashmi too was not unaware of the thoughts that Rajen had about life. For Rabhi everything about Rajen was new. There was not an instance when the hues of Rajen's life and thoughts did not occupy her mind.

Rajen smiled at Rashmi and Rabhi before entering the operation theatre. Rashmi was emotionally overcome but was careful that the oceans in her eyes did not spill over. It was for the first time that Rabhi's eyes displayed concern. She was steadily looking at Rajen, but was lost in deep thoughts. Neither Rashmi nor Rabhi could reciprocate Rajen's smile.

The lights in the operation theatre seemed like the silver lining of the dark clouds. All the equipment was set systematically beside the bed. Dr. Rao was to investigate the ulcer with the state-of-art fiber optic gastroscope.

Rajen was asked to wear a pair of sterile clothes before lying down. An army of nurses and doctors were ready in their own special garb. Dr. Rao too entered from a neighbouring room wearing an operation gown.

Rajen had a look at all the different equipment lying about, the anesthetic trolley, face masks, the IV sets, blood transfusion sets, oxygen cylinders, suction cleaners and the other equipment.

"Sir...since I do not obey your orders while I am awake, so you will anesthetize me, right? Okay...as you please..." saying that, Rajen lay down on the table of the operation theatre.

For one long hour Rabhi and Rashmi paced up and down outside the operation theatre.

"Rajen will be out in some time," Dr. Rao informed Rashmi and Rabhi as he stepped out of the operating theatre. Rajen was still under the influence of drugs and was brought back to Room No. 9 on the stretcher. According to the doctor, Rajen would regain complete consciousness in about four hours. As he regained consciousness, there may be signs of struggle but the instructions were that there was nothing to worry about.

Perhaps for the first time there was total silence in Room No.

9 after such a long spell. Rabhi had not gone home today. Rabhi and Rashmi had waited all the time next to Rajen's bed. Both were fearing that Rajen may get violent any time. To their surprise, Rajen slowly opened his eyes after about five hours without any signs of struggle. He closed his eyes again. Once again he regained consciousness briefly only to fall back into a drugged stupor.

After a couple of such episodes, Rajen complained of nausea. Rabhi was on her feet immediately with a kidney tray which she held close to Rajen's mouth.

Rajen threw up a lot of liquid. There was some blood in it. By now Rajen had regained full consciousness. As per the instructions of the doctor, Rashmi began giving him liquids. The nurses were regularly monitoring his temperature and blood pressure readings.

"Rashmi...has the report arrived?..." Rajen inquired about his gastroscopy report but the report hadn't yet arrived.

Realising that Rabhi had been by his side all through the day, he thanked her. It was quite late but Rabhi did not feel like going home. But after much cajoling by Rajen, she finally left.

≈

With each passing day now Rajen's health began to deteriorate. After the gastroscope examination, a malignancy in the stomach was confirmed. Dr. Rao was careful not to trouble Rajen too often. He had started the chemotherapy and Rajen was being given injections of anti-cancer drugs regularly which were intravenously administered.

Rajen tried hard to continue smiling, but failed to conceal his growing pain.

The deep sunken eyes were because of the strong medicines which he was being given. Rajen had now indeed begun to look like a patient on the brink of death.

Rabhi started spending all her time with Rajen. Because of Rabhi, Rashmi was relieved of a great deal of pressure. The closeness between Rajen and Rabhi had grown. Rajen wanted that Rabhi should always be near him.

He would inquire after Rabhi even if she left for short intervals.

Without Rajen's knowledge, Rabhi had sought other medical opinions for Rajen's condition. Rabhi toiled day after day so that Rajen may live. Even when she was away, she always remained with Rajen in spirit. She was unable to understand why she felt so deeply for Rajen. Her only prayer was to save Rajen from death.

Rajen could now hardly eat anything. He looked emaciated. Dr. Rao had now initiated cobalt radiotherapy. He was taken regularly for the radiation sessions. Rajen had lost so much weight that Rabhi alone could lift him and move him on to the stretcher.

After being exposed to the rays he would get some relief from the pain but later would suffer from a burning sensation all through his body. As soon as Rajen complained of this, Rabhi would massage his body gently. Rabhi had started serving Rajen with all her heart and mind, he had become the center point of her very existence.

As soon as he recovered a little, Rajen tried to show his element but nowadays there was no soul in his mischief. Sometimes in jest, he would tell her, "Rabhi, my mischievous ways seem to have died before me." Rajan was depressed realizing that his dream of being carefree till death would remain just a dream.

≈

"Rabhi, I am feeling a little better today. It would be so nice if I could go out with you for a short walk..." Rajen requested her with the innocence of a child.

Rajen put a hand on Rabhi's shoulders and started walking slowly, taking small, unsteady steps. Rabhi's daily meeting with the other patients with her roses was still pending. As she walked with Rajen, she tended to the other patients as well. Looking at her loving routine with the other patients, Rajen smiled inwardly.

Rabhi handed a rose to a child suffering from cancer of the eye, in special room no. 17 which was reserved for children. As she affectionately cuddled her Rabhi was just like a child while she played with that kid.

A few moments later Rabhi suddenly looked downcast and sad. It took Rajen by surprise. Rabhi pulled out another rose and placed it on the bed. Rabhi's head was bowed down. Her face had a somber look. Rabhi stood there quietly for some time. It was the first occasion for Rajen to see Rabhi in such a mood. It was only when Rajen shook Rabhi lightly by her shoulder that she realised that Rajen was still there with her.

Rabhi made an effort to regain her composure as she walked further giving support to Rajen. Rajen could not understand this. He could not remain silent for long. "Rabhi...Room No. 17...your getting upset there quite suddenly...Rabhi, I cannot fathom. If you don't mind..." Rajen gently tried to ask her the reason for her torment, "Not at all Rajen...why should I mind...?" saying that she began to tell her story.

"Rajen, Room No. 17 had this handsome teenager, hardly fifteen, who had come here to wrap up his life. He was very dear to each in his family. That boy was very loving, full of mirth, affection and left a lasting impression on my mind. I had worked very hard just so that he may live longer but..." Rabhi stopped speaking as her eyes glistened with tears.

"He was so loving that anyone would instantly start liking him, perhaps that was the reason that God needed him more."

As soon as she was composed she began again, "He had made

a last dying wish. Rabhididi, will you put a rose here even after I leave?...he had said"

"Rajen, it's only to fulfill his wish, that I put these two flowers there" Rabhi's mind was enveloped in these memories of the past.

Rabhi's life brimming with affection for all was leaving a deep impression on Rajen's soul.

~

During the last couple of days, vomiting blood had become a routine for Rajen. Rajen was getting blood transfusion nearly everyday. Inspite of the doctors' refusal Rabhi had donated her blood twice in the last few weeks.

Rajen was unable to eat now. The doctors had punctured a hole in Rajen's abdomen and were feeding him with the pint method.

Rajen's nose and throat were connected to suction machines. There were times when he became very breathless. With a rumbling sound the machine would clean up the insides of Rajen's throat and lungs. It was clear that Rajen may not live much longer. Everyone around could see that.

~

Rabhi had, as a routine chore, sponged Rajen clean and dressed him up in crisp new clothes. Today his temperature reading was a little lower. The bedsheets on his bed were also new. Rajen was not feeling well but was repeatedly trying to speak with Rabhi.

At a slow pace, in broken words, he said the most unexpected :

"Rabhi, I have lost the battle."

"How?" Rabhi tried to extend the conversation with a brief reply.

"Till this day, I had always spoken about death comfortably. I had never feared death. Somehow, now I feel like living. I have never differentiated between life and death. And now I love life more. Rabhi...is this not Rajen's biggest defeat? Rabhi...I know well that I may be here just for a few hours more and still I have this feeling, why is this happening?"

Rabhi had no answers except silence. Rabhi's spirit was inquiring - How unfortunate is this moment, when Rajen spoke of death I spoke of life and now that he is speaking about life and living, I do not have anything to offer him except my silence.

"Perhaps Rabhi, this maybe our last conversation."

Hearing this Rabhi's emotions found a way out through her eyes.

"Rabhi, you drop two roses in room no. 17 don't you...?"

"Yes"

"Just to fulfill that boy's death wish...then Rabhi...would you not care to...fulfill just one wish...of mine?"

Rajen was speaking as if his time was running out, without a pause and looking straight into Rabhi's eyes.

"Yes Rajen...any wish that you may have..."

Before she could complete, Rajen began to speak again :

"Rabhi... you live for the sake of others, isn't it? You have remained single just for that... I have just one wish... Rabhi would you not get married? Rabhi, not for your happiness but for my wish... Rabhi, just for Rajen's wish would you marry?"

It was after a long time Rajen's eyes were shining brightly.

Rabhi was unable to comprehend what was going on. How can I tell him.. How would he feel?

"Rabhi, you are an epitome of affection... just for that... Rabhi could you fulfill this wish...?"

Rajen was repeatedly inquiring in expectation of an

answer.

"But...what?" Rabhi's query increased his eagerness.

"Rabhi...I am... hardly...here...now for a few hours, however if you get married, I only wish that I may be born of you as your son...it is my fervent wish. Would you not take me and give birth to me of you as your son? Just for this.. would you marry?

"Please Rabhi...just one wish that I have..."

Rajen's body was now throbbbing. His breathing had quick-ened. Rajen held Rabhi's hand tightly. His eyes were looking deep into Rabhi's eyes. Rajen was covered with perspiration. It was getting difficult for Rajen to utter even a single word. His eyes had nothing but expectation of an answer.

Rajen's wish had touched upon the motherhood nesting in a woman's heart. Rabhi was gently rubbing her hand on Rajen's hand.

For a long time Rabhi could not look at Rajen. "Rajen, I will fulfill your wish," Rabhi replied, her tears of affection flowing freely.

With Rabhi's answer Rajen's body was getting colder. He was trying to say something but couldn't. His eyes were in some kind of a spasm. His grip over her hand was loosening.

Rajen gestured that he wanted to throw up. Before Rabhi could get hold of the kidney tray he vomited blood. Never before had he vomited so much blood. Rabhi's rose was drenched in the blood.

Rajen became unconscious. The doctors administered coramine injections to revive him. The suction machines were switched on to clear the obstructions coming in the way of his respiration. The doctors gave him a cardiac massage...

For the last time Rajen opened his eyes and had a last look at Rabhi.. and his head flopped on to his side. The walls of Room

No. 9 that had recently learned to laugh were silently sobbing now.

~

Just as her earlier routine, Rabhi walked into the hospital today too. She stopped at Room No. 9. The basket of roses that she held in her hand slid on to the floor and out fell the roses. A thought raced through her mind : "Behold! Here a life has set, igniting a hope of the rise of another..."

Rabhi could go no further. With a heavy heart she turned back. She saw Rashmi standing before her.

"Rabhi..now this job is mine.." Saying this she started picking up the roses from the floor and putting them back into the basket.

Critique

The psalm of the power of motherhood 'Room No. 9'

*Balvant Jani**

In the process of the study of language, we have been able to enjoy the fruit in the form of thoughtful prose and sensitive poetry. However, there are very few who know that Mr. Narendra Modi has written profound and sensitive stories. His wide reading of literature, an unending desire to nurture the value system of a nation, and deep understanding of the problems faced by the society had motivated Narendrabhai to write some stories which were first printed some time ago but are being brought in a book form only now. With the literary understanding of Gunvantbhai Shah, Gopalbhai Makadia's passion to publish meaningful literature along with appreciative and critical inputs from friends like us, I am sure all this will go a long way in establishing it as a valuable work.

When I first read the title of this story I was reminded of the famous story by Chekhov, 'Ward No. 6'. However that story recounts the travails of the mind of a psychiatrist who works in an asylum, whereas this story opens up the floodgates of the psychological facets of the Indian way of living and the associated value system by presenting the facets of the power of motherhood.

The hero of the story is Rajen, a cancer patient, full of joy and mirth who keeps everyone away from his own and private sorrow. He drives his own car while going to the hospital to get admitted there. When admitted in Room No. 9 he infects the entire hospital with joy, not just

---

* Well known Gujarati reviewer

his own room. The principle of his life was : Life is death for the people who fear death. Death too likes the company of such people. Inspite of strict instructions to rest, he inquires about the health of others. He tells Dr. Rao, "The ambience here is so peaceful and serene which makes me feel that even dying here would be enjoyable."

He tells Rabhi who offers roses to the patients, "This is true for the patients here too. I know well that just like the rose I too will wilt...The only reason I wish to dedicate compassion, mirth... to them...actually strive to drench them in it!"

Rajen would much rather walk than take the stretcher on way to the operation theatre. He knows about his impending end and yet does not lose hope. Of course he does mention it to Rabhi, with whom he has an emotional bonding "Rabhi, I have lost the battle...I have never differentiated between life and death...And now I love life more."

When Rajen, the hero of the story requests Rabhi to promise him that she would marry, so that he may be born of her, the reader is jolted.

- However, the basis of Rajen's life are - The three women who are the supreme examples of the power of motherhood like the abode of love.

Who are these three women?

a) Mother

Most of the stories in this collection have the description of mother as an epitome of love. The supreme form of a woman is the mother. Mr. Narendra Modi describes Rajen's mother in just a few words.

When Rajen eulogized Rashmi for her dedication - "Rabhi, if I have an opportunity to paint a picture combining labour, the spirit of surrender and faith it would definitely look like Rashmi..."

To which Rabhi asks, "Oh! Rajen, so you are a painter?"

To which he answers, "She was an epitome of love. When Mother was dying I hated having her to die, it was unbearable for me. However, today I feel what happened was for good...that she departed earlier..."

It is as if Mr. Narendra Modi is paying homage to all the mothers of this universe.

b) Rashmi

As soon as Rajen stops the car at the hospital he refers to the 'destination' which does not go well with Rashmi : She corrects him

"No…Bro…just an encampment." The emotional sister then breaks down.

This sister has tended her endearing brother since the beginning and continues to do so with the same sincerety. Rajen introduces his sister with these words : "One who has never deprived me of anything that I may wish for..." and "you are fortunate to have such a sister."

The author expresses the feelings of a kid sister who takes on the role of a sister and a mother as well to her elder brother with such finesse. The sister later on continues her role of a sacrificing and loving person even after her brother's death. She makes every effort to save her brother from death, and continues to do so even after his death to the extent that she takes over from Rabhi the job of offering roses to the patients.

c) The social worker Rabhi who offers flowers.

This story with wonderful hues of emotions, which has evolved from the pen of the author truly touches the heart. It goes without saying that such a story can be penned only by one who himself has gone through plenty of emotional upheavals. Spreading the fragrance of a rose among the patients who are nearing their end and fill their days with warmth and hope could easily be considered to be unparalleled.

When Rajen was admitted to Room No. 9, she sweetly calls out with a handful of roses "May I come in?" A woman with striking looks and hardly about twenty five or less; seemingly from a good family, who had an attractive smile on her face, who had an imposing person- ality, where nature had been very kind in moulding her frame that was Rabhi.

Rabhi gets involved with this wonderful patient in the very first meeting. Her routine was to fill all the cancer patients' hearts with warmth and happiness by offering them roses. Even Rajen had similar qualities. He knew that death is close by and still he tried to embrace all those around him with warmth. Rabhi was immersed in social service and her only joy lay in the serving the ailing.

She gets upset when Rajen is being taken to the operation theatre. She and Rashmi wait upon the unconscious Rajen. Now it seemed that Rajen was about to die. He expresses his defeat and says, "Rabhi, my mischievous ways seem to have died before me."

Even in such a condition he limps up to the pediatric ward no.

17 with Rabhi's support. Rabhi suddenly becomes sad while giving away the roses, because she recollects a 15 years old boy who had died there after making a wish that she should drop a rose on his bed even after his death: "Rabhididi, will you drop a rose here even after I leave?"

The dialogues between Rajen and Rabhi when he is on his deathbed are matchless in expressing the climaxing of affection : "I only wish that I may be born of you as your son...it is my fervent wish. Would you not take me and give birth to me as your son?"

"Rajen, I will fulfill your wish."

Here Rabhi displays lofty heights of emotions that only a human being can be capable of.

Then Rajen's body starts getting cold, the bloody vomits, the drenching of one of the roses in the blood...about the walls of Room No.9 sobbing inconsolably...

The storyteller Narendra Modi's pen spouts a striking sentence: "Behold! Here a life has set, igniting a hope of the rise of another..."

I have not read all the stories from the collection 'Abode of Love', but I can say this that though these stories were published in magazines as *Aaraam* and *Chandani* have remained as fresh as Rabhi's roses.

When these stories are published, it shall be known to Gujarat that Chief Minister Narendra Modi is also an able and capable storyteller. His language is simple, pointed and profound. The flow in his stories never diminishes. There are no sermons. Even if most of the characters are women or mothers who are endowed with great dedication, there is a great deal of variety in building the characters and emotions. It is because of the parameters of the power of motherhood which are depicted here that one feels like describing it as a psalm of the power of motherhood.

My publisher and friend Gopalbhai Makadia deserves to be congratulated for he let it out that "Mr. Narendra Modi is a capable storyteller." I wish to thank this avatar of Mr. Narendra Modi as a storyteller and finally wish to inquire - 'Could Narendrabhai not have been able to write such fine stories while serving as the Chief Minister?'

The Lamp

The Lamp

Everyone was there when they got together to break Radha's glass bangles. The dark black clothes she wore were new but seemed to hang on her lean frame. Radha's life was enveloped in the darkness as black and drab as her clothes. She stood up to walk but missed a step and almost fell.

Their life of togetherness had just about begun but Kanji had wrapped up his existence too soon.

The chronic illness had forced Kanji to surrender before death.

But for Radha it was not just Kanji who had died, her very life seemed to have been extinguished.

All the while Kanji was fighting death, Radha had been his only source of comfort.

This is what drove everyone in the house into mercilessly taunting Radha on every occasion.

They threw barbs at her, mocking her to the point that it slaughtered Radha's very being, her aspirations, and her sensibilities.

Kanji had been unemployed and worthless for the family while alive.

Radha well knew that the family did not really care whether Kanji lived or died. And now they were merely taking care just as one would for any dead body.

Radha had no other alternative, but to bear the cruel words and the pain.

As she slowly moved towards Kanji's body, Radha's mind was a whirlpool of thoughts...

Her heart was ceaselessly crying out, "Kanji has died, but he wanted to live...he was nearly coerced to die inspite of a will to live."

Radha's eyes were fixated on Kanji's lifeless body.

Everyone in the household was busy arranging the last rites. Radha felt as if he was still begging for life.

Kanji's mother lit a lamp near his lifeless body. It was customary to keep the lamp burning until the funeral rites were over.

Radha was frustrated to see the earthen bowl containing the lamp full of *ghee* (clarified butter). Nobody in the house had cared to give him even a spoonful of *ghee* to take his medicines with and here was an earthen bowl filled brimful with *ghee*, just to light a lamp near his lifeless body!

Radha's heart and mind were consumed by a cold numbness.

As Kanji's body was being taken away for the funeral, Radha who had not shed a tear till then suddenly started sobbing uncontrollably. Crying, she collapsed at the very spot where Kanji's body had been kept, accidentally extinguishing the earthen bowl lamp which had been burning beside Kanji's lifeless body.

"You whore, chicken brain, may you burn in the fires of hell, can't you see...you just put off the lamp, you idiot!" Kanji's mother ranted at Radha, spewing the worst possible profanities imaginable.

But by then Radha had lost all her senses unable to hear even a single profanity that was being directed at her.

Critique

'The Lamp'–A work giving a brief idea about the status of women in Indian society

Dr. Bipin Ashar*

As a reviewer it has been my experience that two types of creations are always the most challenging ones: First, those which are very brief and seemingly without a message and second, those which seem too simple. The comparison between the two types is of a different genre. The duty of the reviewer with reference to complex and convoluted works should surely be to present the complexities of the work in such a manner that the concealed and latent elements should be pinpointed so as to enhance their appreciation. The question is about examining the simple and straightforward works which do not measure up to the levels of a true literary form. My approach has always been to point out the best in each work, though the work itself may not be the best. This approach has been adopted because I realize that it may not be the aim of all who create, to write something that stands scrutiny as a remarkable work of literature and the author be spoken of as a litterateur. It is indeed, a fact that for some of the authors, writing has been only a medium of expressing their emotions. In the midst of such creators Narendra Modi is a name that surprises many. He is the Chief Minister of our state of Gujarat, Mr. Narendra Modi.

One of the stories 'The Lamp' which Narendra Modi had written about three decades ago is kept before me to be savoured. It is really not worth deliberating if this very brief work should be classified as a

_____
* Well known Gujarati reviewer

short story. This tale is hardly reviewable; rather it is fit to be absorbed on a canvas of the reader's emotions. The author's sensitivities, upheavals in his thinking, and his minute observations of the typically Indian societal customs and psyches of the people is enough proof of the fact that it will spark off the readers' sensitivities and push them to think deeper. It reminds me that short stories have often been described as "epiphanies" or "pieces of perception".

This creation contains the elements of perception and the thought behind it. The central idea of this story is the "death of the husband". Even if death is universal and everlasting, it touches each person in many different ways.

When Radha and Kanji are separated by death, an unseasoned pen tries to create a picture of words in a way that arouses emotions within the readers' hearts about the turmoil that sets in the life of Radha from within and without. The story starts with a narrative that describes the Indian social customs and the tragic state of Radha.

"Everyone was there when they got together to break Radha's glass bangles. The dark black clothes she wore were new and seemed to hang on her lean frame. Radha's life was enveloped in the darkness as black and drab as her clothes. She stood up to walk but missed a step and almost fell."

The most tragic episode in any Indian woman's life is arguably the death of her husband. The husband's death brings about radical changes in the life of an Indian woman. A society which believes that the death of the husband brings a woman's life to an end, snatches away all the rights of a woman and puts a big full stop on any happiness which she may deserve. Only an Indian married woman can truly appreciate the worth of the "glass bangles". There could be umpteen occasions that glass bangles could break but its only once that they are deliberately broken. New clothes and bright colours are the mani-festations of happiness; in contrast the new clothes which are dark and black are suggestive of misfortune. While a woman, who had been strutting in colourful clothes, has to wear a brand new black garb, it symbolizes the unfortunate state of that woman where it seems to "hang" on her body. How does she feel then? One who has been nimbly dancing her way through life finds herself unable to move. She "misses" a step and is on the verge of falling down. That this particular emotional state of an Indian woman is represented not just with brevity but that it has only casually been pointed out is indicative of the craft with which this story is written. Along with the author, the reader too assumes that Radha is indeed under a shadow of misfortune. The only difference between the reader and the author is that he records this situation in the form of a simile.

"Radha's life was enveloped in the darkness as black and drab as her clothes."

While the lamp shines, it is a source of uninterrupted light, but as soon as it dims, the darkness takes over. The husband is a 'lamp' in an Indian woman's life. The presence of the husband is enough to light up the woman's life. Only Indian woman can truly realize and suffer the consequences of the reality of losing a husband. The author tries to point out this distinguishing characteristic in just a few lines.

The author has linked the references to the couple's married life and the family to reveal the critical aspects of the story in the concise manner of an aerial surveillance of an area struck with some natural disaster. The sentence "Their life of togetherness had just begun" indicates that they married rather recently. Perhaps some four decades of togetherness may not be as painful, but Radha is facing widowhood at a very young age. It is extremely difficult for an Indian woman to become a young widow. Radha is witnessing these difficult times. Her husband Kanji had died of a long drawn out illness. She had served and cared for him during his concluding days as a life partner would. She had injected strength into him to fight death. However, for the other members of the family, Kanji had been useless, because he was unemployed and did not bring home money. Using this family as an instrument, the author has exposed the selfish ways of a self centred society by revealing that the one who earns well is the jewel in the crown of the family. When the man of the house does not contribute to the home's earning, his wife is always in a despicable condition. Here the husband is unemployed and sick. Radha who is suffering the outcome of such an unfortunate combination of circumstances, has been performing the duties of a wife to the best of her ability. The family on the other hand too seems to follow their own peculiar set of duties by mocking and degrading her. Her situation which is sandwiched between the husband's illness and the family's hatred is truly pathetic. In these circumstances when the man dies it does not come as a shock for the family. The story describes Radha's mental condition with the help of a string of events which shows the man's will to live, inhuman actions of the family members, and Kanji's death. By pointing towards the treatment meted out by the family towards Kanji, the author has brought to light a social truth in some sections of the society.

The inescapable characteristic of this story is the summarized version of the activities and nature of the Indian mindset. The Indian mindset has always been moulded in such a manner that it can believe and act in any manner in the name of religious beliefs. A family which has hardly cared for the living Kanji, is now occupied with the act of carrying out the funeral as per the customary norms. A lamp has been kept burning next to his lifeless body. While looking at the amount of *ghee* (clarified butter) being poured into the earthen bowl which contains the wick of the lamp, feelings are expressed in the following manner: "Radha was frustrated to see the earthen bowl containing the lamp, full of *ghee*. None in the house had cared to give him a spoonful of *ghee* to take his medicines with and here was an earthen bowl filled with *ghee*, like it was there to cremate him." This reflection is a little different than what they say, "Poor men's reasons are not heard, and the rich need not give a reason." In this reference, it is natural that I am reminded of the remarkable story 'Godaan' by one of the greatest storytellers in Hindi, Munshi Premchand. A common labourer wishes to own a cow, but is unable to do so even after working hard for it. After his death, the priest asks his wife to donate a cow for the liberation of his soul. The Indian woman braves many difficulties and succeeds in donating a cow for the sake of her dead husband.

Here Radha contemplates upon the amount of *ghee* used for burning the lamp bringing to light the hypocrisy in the behaviour of the family members. The author thus notes the importance of the social customs for the dead in comparison to a living being.

There has been much speculation how a story should end. The story in question has an expected end. The remarkable attribute of this very short story which emerges is the heartlessness of the family and the position of the Indian woman in the family system found somewhere in India. The funeral procession is on its way and when that happens, the firmly composed Radha cannot take it anymore and bursts out crying. She is dizzy while she cries and falls down extinguishing the lamp. The mother-in-law starts spouting the most degrading profanities that are possible upon Radha :

"You whore, chicken brain, may you burn in the fires of hell...can't you see...you just put off the lamp, you idiot!"

It is the same Indian woman who does not have the sensitivity to realize that it is her own son who has died, when she is in a role of a mother-in-law. Only an Indian woman knows how a mother-in-law can address her daughter-in-law. The author has tried to put forth the Indian mindset and the position of a particular Indian woman. Radha was not even in her senses while the mother-in-law eulogizes her with such a rich collection of expletives. It is true that women down the ages have been using such expletives and women have also been hearing them. I doubt if even the twenty first century has brought about any significant change in this context.

The title 'The Lamp' is justified on two counts. Firstly, the husband of Radha has lost his life, the metaphorical comparison with the lamp and about the darkness that has covered Radha's life. Secondly, when the lamp beside Kanji's body gets extinguished this hurt the religious sentiments of the mother-in-law which give rise to the angry outburst. At this point the lamp symbolizes the light of the soul which is lost in the darkness.

With the permeation of the western way of life, it seems that the Indian society is inclining towards materialistic ways. It is time that we identify the true form of our culture, and do not allow the superstitions that have been embedded so deeply in our psyches to destroy our thinking faculty, our discretion and emotional identity. Only then will many such works including 'The Lamp' and the effort put in by the author in writing it be justified.

The most beautiful word that mankind can speak is mother and the most beautiful sound that may be cried out is "My mother". A word full of sweetness and affection that comes from the depths of the heart. The mother is everything - she is our consolation in sorrow, our hope in misery, and our strength in weakness. She is the source of love, mercy, sympathy, and forgiveness. One who loses her, loses a pure soul that continually showers blessings upon him.

Everything in nature has motherhood in it. The sun is the mother of earth and feeds it with sunshine. It does not depart from the earth until the music of the oceans and the birds and the singing streams do not lull it into sweet sleep. The earth itself is the mother of the trees and the flowers. They are born out of her, they grow upon her and these trees and the fruits and flowers give birth to their seeds. And the Mother, the primordial form of all that exists is an infinite soul full of beauty and love.

—**Kahlil Gibran**

Bridge

Bridge

Sounds of the chirping crickets and croaking frogs were drowning out the sound of the heavy rain. Surbhi *bhabhi* was fed up waiting for the luxury of getting some sleep. Her mind was numb. She could not fathom the reason for her wakeful state.

All through the night she got up several times with a start just to look at Setu. Affectionately she ran her hand over Setu's head and occasionally planted kisses all over his face.

The night passed, but sleep eluded her. Tired of tossing and turning Surbhi *bhabhi* wearily got out of bed. In the hope of diverting her mind she busied herself in the routines of the morning chores. She had no idea of the time. In any case when the cycle of life has stopped, it hardly matters whether or not the clock take its roundabout route.

The darkness of that night was heightening the sorrow of her heart drifting in the dark waters of her life. Each moment was turning into a fresh torment beyond her tolerance. She woke Setu up early in the hope that his prattle would provide her with some relief, but of no avail. Even before the sun's rays could bathe the planet, she had finished getting Setu dressed.

There were so many questions popping up in Setu's mind, "Oh why Mother, why so early?" However, he sensed his mother's behaviour accompanied by her dignified silence, and did not have the courage to ask again.

Silence filled the room - a dull and flavourless silence. It did not have the radiance which emanates from a tranquil lake when it reflects the first rays of the sun. Rather, there was solemnity, pain, and parchedness. There were tears. There was silence but no peace!

There was silence because there were no words. The lack of words was because the very fervour that could have expressed the ravaging thoughts, was absent. When it becomes too difficult for the pain to express itself in words, it translates into silence. A vessel full of sorrow brims with tears. Surbhi *bhabhi*'s state was similar. She could no longer hold back her tears. While running a comb through her hair, she faced the mirror and lifted up Setu close to her bosom. The tears fell on Setu's cheeks. Setu's face looked even more beautiful just like a fresh flower covered with morning dew.

"What's wrong with Mother today?" the question was repeating itself in Setu's mind, but he could not get himself to ask. He wanted to weep but he could not let himself do it.

As soon as she heard the milkman's cry, Surbhi *bhabhi* wiped her tears and came out of the house to get the milk. But she realized that she had reacted too soon, the milkman was still at the far end of the street. She understood that she was not her normal self and yet was unable to control her thoughts. As she waited for the milkman to arrive at her doorstep, she was back to her solitary self, floating on her raft of thoughts in a desolate sea.

"So prompt today...ma'am? ...How much?" the milkman inquired in his distinctive rustic way. Without waiting for an answer for his opening query, he did not waste time in coming to the point. Hearing this Surbhi *bhabhi* woke up from her daze.

Setu was familiar with the ways of his mother. Today, however, he was wondering why his mother was so upset. It was gnawing at his conscience as he followed her around the house.

Setu was dressed in a white pajama and a kurta, so Surbhi *bhabhi* asked him to stay away from the kitchen lest the white clothes get soiled. But Setu was not ready to be shooed away; he stood there facing his mother. Surbhi *bhabhi* looked long at Setu while she was busy igniting the kerosene stove and as if without her knowledge, she again started running her hand over his head. Setu was the focus of all her activities. She had no dreams of her own but was determined to fulfill Sohan's dreams. Today these feelings were getting fiercer.

Just as the lowest portion of the milk in the vessel on the kerosene stove was sweeping up towards the brim, so were the emotional upheavals rising in her heart. They were spreading towards Setu's future. Surbhi *bhabhi*'s being was caught in a tight knot of feelings, which she had never once experienced in the bygone year.

Her mind continued to stray in the past. There were moments when Sohan's face flashed before her followed by Setu's. Surbhi *bhabhi*, engrossed in this rapidly alternating mental images, remembered distinctly Sohan's words : "Surbhi, are you aware why I like our son's name - Setu?" Surbhi *bhabhi* could still visualize the confidence on his face, with which Sohan answered his own question.

"Not for him to act as a bridge between Sohan and Surbhi or that he would be an instrument for our happiness.

"Or that he becomes a mirror of our expressions or of our ambitions? I only hope that he be a representative of a generation strongly bridging our marvellous past and a bright future...and thus a bridge...Setu! Just love that name. As you know, the meaning of the word setu is bridge."

Surbhi *bhabhi* felt that her beloved Sohan's words were turning out to be a grave responsibility on her shoulders.

Sohan too had lived amongst the dreams of a marvellous past and a bright future. Sohan's brief life had left an indelible impression on Surbhi, which was quite apparent.

Why just the way he lived? Even the way he died. Did he not embrace death for the same.

Not for his personal aspirations, but for the ideals.

It was not for the happiness but for the sake of service.

His desire to carry on with his responsibilities had been the reason of his death.

Pondering upon Sohan's words, she was reminded of the tragic episode of the darkest hour of her life. Exactly a year ago on this very day... It was Gurupurnima. Sohan dressed himself in white and readied for the rituals in reverence of his guru from whom he had imbibed all the goodness, and his ideals. Setu and Surbhi had accompanied him to the doorstep when they heard some loud commotion. Sohan forgot about his programme for the day and rushed towards the direction of the noise.

There was a big crowd at the temple. Thousands from the neighbouring villages had flocked to seek blessings of the guru. A great bamboo structure had been erected at the site of the ancient, crumbling temple for the devotees. But the structure could not take the weight of so many devotees and crashed with a big thud. Loud screams could be heard. Even before the screams had subsided, Sohan was at the site, making his way through the crowd towards the fallen debris of the broken wooden structure. Many had been buried below the debris. Some of them had serious injuries. There were people who were crushed in the stampede that followed.

Sohan began efforts to rescue as many as he possibly could. There were others who followed suit and gave a helping hand to Sohan. Each of them in that crowd was trying to escape death. In their desperation to escape, they had jumped out from the rear and climbed on the roof to get some air in their lungs. There was a very big crowd already on the roof, it was doubtful that the roof of that ancient temple could hold the weight of these people. The roof collapsed taking the hundreds along with it to the ground. A large beam from the roof fell and hit Sohan on his head and he fell to the ground. The story she had heard from the eyewitnesses was reconstructing itself before her eyes.

The news about Sohan hit her like a bolt of lightning. She flung Setu on her shoulders and ran towards the temple. It was not Sohan who was extracted from the wreck, only his lifeless body. It took great courage for her to approach Sohan's body. His face had a content look of having completed his duty. Surbhi *bhabhi* was in shock. It was a blow which annihilated her soul. Even her tears were hard to come by.

Surbhi *bhabhi*'s spirit said - Sohan lived for the society and died for it.

Sohan was no more. She was now living just for the sake of his dreams. His dream was Setu.

Surbhi *bhabhi* called out for Setu and asked him to bring a small *kalash*. This *kalash* had been Setu's friend for the last one year. Mother would regularly give him five and ten paise coins to drop into it. Once he was tempted to use some of that loose change. His mother had explained that he could not since all that money was to be sent to his father. After that Setu never had a similar urge again. That was not all, he even put the coins which guests gave him as gifts into the *kalash*.

As he handed the *kalash* to his mother, he could not resist asking her, "Is this going to be sent to Papa today?" She had no answer for him. She could only look down and say nothing.

Surbhi *bhabhi* made Setu put a tiny garland of flowers around the neck of the pitcher. She then asked him to shower it with some 'kumkum' and rice grains. On a white cloth she made him write a mantra with the red kumkum powder.

"*Rashtriya svaha, rastriya idam na mum?*"
(Oblation to the nation, it belongs to the nation, not me)
And then tied the cloth on the mouth of the *kalash*. It was

a mantra very close to Sohan's heart. It was this mantra, which he had adopted as the motto of his life. Surbhi *bhabhi* had the satisfaction of making Setu follow his father's ideals, of directing him along his father's footsteps.

Surbhi *bhabhi* reached the outskirts of the village and started to walk towards some hutments. The surprised Setu asked her,"Mother, does Papa stay here? You had said that we will send this money to Papa!"

"No...your Papa's dreams lie scattered somewhere here. I want you to meet them." She said all of this without realizing how much of it would he really understand.

Everyone in those hutments was watching the duo. Of course, Surbhi *bhabhi* was no stranger to this place, but Setu's visit was something unexpected for them. They watched him anxiously and expectantly. Surbhi *bhabhi* stopped near two children standing on a doorway. Both children had an expression of meeting a confidante.

The people who had died with Sohan included the parents of these children. When Sohan's body was discovered, he had held the hand of this child's father. Surbhi had assumed and taken upon herself the unfinished task of Sohan by holding hands of the orphaned children of an unfortunate father. These children would visit Surbhi *bhabhi*'s residence quite often and knew Setu well.

As soon as they saw Setu, they beamed brightly. Under Surbhi's instructions, Setu marked their foreheads with the kumkum. Without waiting he picked the *kalash* from his Mother's hands and handed it to the two children. Everything happened very spontaneously. Seeing the moist eyes of these children Setu burst into tears releasing the heavy weight which had been building up in his heart since morning.

Surbhi *bhabhi* who had been melancholy since morning smiled contentedly for the first time.

Critique

"Bridge"–bridging our marvellous past and a bright future

*Hasmukh Rawal**

It is not about the bridge, which joins the parents in the form of a son. It is also not the bridge used as an instrument for the happiness and prosperity of the parents. It is also not about the bridge that becomes an expression of personal aspirations.

Sohan, one who has sacrificed his life while trying to save many other lives says : "I only hope that he be a representative of a generation strongly bridging our marvellous past and a bright future...and thus a bridge..Setu! Just love that name."

Setu is the son of late Sohan and Surbhi. The widowed wife reminiscencs, "Sohan too had lived amongst the dreams of a marvellous past and a bright future."

It has been one year since the death of Sohan. It is not just the restlessness and grief that has been weighing on Surbhi's being, but while she watches her son Setu it also awakens a chain of indelible memories in her mind.

The sixth story of this sensitive collection of short stories 'Abode of Love' by Mr. Narendra Modi is the tale of a mother, a wife; a stirring story involving an affectionate woman's emotional upheavals and orientation towards the service of humanity.

The author has succeeded in painting so many pictures with just a few strokes of his brush.

---

* Well known Gujarati columnist and novelist

- Sounds of the chirping crickets and croaking frogs were drowning out the sound of heavy rain. Surbhi *bhabhi* was fed up of waiting for the luxury of getting some sleep.

- Affectionately she ran her hand over Setu's head and occasionally planted kisses all over his face.

After the accidental death of Sohan, the works of service, which she must have undertaken, remain unspoken of by the author. However, this fact is evident from the name Surbhi *bhabhi* with which the villagers address her.

Surbhi spends an emotionally charged night with great difficulty and wakes Setu up early the next morning. Setu, then does not dare to converse with his mother seeing her lost in her own work.

- A vessel full of sorrow brims with tears.

Looking at her tears, Setu begins to think,"What's wrong with Mother today?"

Surbhi perennially struggles to fulfill Sohan's dreams, because— "Her soul continued to stray in the past unintentionally."

The flashback illustrating the dialogue between the couple, Sohan's ideas about Setu and "His desire to carry on with his responsibilities had been the reason of his death" portrays a nice technique to convey a message. It climaxes at "It was not Sohan who was extracted from the wreck, only his lifeless body."

The author summarizes :

Sohan was no more. It was worth living just for the sake of his dreams. His dream was Setu.

It has been a whole year since Sohan died.

When Surbhi *bhabhi* asks Setu to fetch the *kalash* full of money, Setu asks innocently :

"Is this going to be sent to Papa today?"

The garland on the *kalash*, showering of kumkum and rice grains on the mouth of the pitcher and scribbling the mantra with Setu's angelic hands :

"*Rashtriya svaha, rashtriya idam na mum*"

Sohan's favourite mantra.

Then it was her visit to the hutments, where there were children whose parents had taken their heavenly course along with Sohan.

- Without waiting, he picked the *kalash* from his Mother's hands handing it to the two children.

- Surbhi *bhabhi* who had been melancholy since morning saw herself contentedly smiling for the first time.

Mr. Narendra Modi as an author of this story successfully touches the hearts of his readers more than once.

The author offers his homage to an affectionate mother, a sensitive and loving spouse and a woman dedicated to serve the masses all at once.

After the demise of her husband, with 'Setu' as an instrument of karma, the process of her becoming Surbhi`bhabhi' for the villagers is depicted sensitively in a lucid style by the author. The sensitivities of the author are obvious.

In this story that was written many years ago, do you as a contemporary reader hear the echoing mantra *Rashtriya svaha, rashtriya idam na mum.*

There came an occasion after twelve years of renouncing the world that I found my mother standing before me. My brother in religion was seated beside me. The mother's heart was spilling with bliss, eyes brimming with tears of joy. I could recognize her, but both of us being in the garb of ascetics she could not recognize which one was her son. When she was told who her son was, she tried to run her hand on my head, inspite of being informed that even the mother or the sister of a Jain ascetic could not touch him. All efforts to contain her failed. Her grievance was : "Even while she lived, why could she not put her hand on her son's head with affection? I have given him birth. I have brought him up for seven years. No one can take away my right to touch him."

When I remember this duel between the religious tenets and mother's love, my heart gets restless.

—Muni Sushilkumar

Igniting Values

Igniting Values

The western way of life came naturally to Jharna. It was not as if she had been born with a silver spoon in her mouth; it was only recently that her family had accumulated a substantial amount of wealth. With it, most in the family had acquired their share of an "elite" group of friends. Their efforts to be looked upon as qualified members of the modern society had met with reasonable success. It was quite evident that Jharna's nouveau rich family could not discern between the lines dividing westernization and modernism.

Whether it be the importance of culture or etiquette or that of the society or the night-life they enjoyed, it hardly mattered.

What is more important, culture or etiquette? What is more important, social norms or club-life? Is wealth more important than contentment? Is religion just a grand temple within the confines of a home or is religion a temple enshrined in your deeds? Does a fleet of fancy cars or a skyscraper define greatness, or is it defined by great deeds? Does grooming accentuate your looks and personality or is it only for shielding your nakedness?

Making their way in the dense forest of such thoughts and contemplation like many other nouveau rich families, Jharna's family had struggled to be called 'forward' rather than 'mediocre'. It was within such a so-called 'forward' society Jharna had grown up.

It was not difficult for the recently wealthy father of Jharna to get her admitted in a good college. For the nouveau rich families especially it mattered greatly which college their children attended as that was a symbol of their standing in society. It also meant that spending big money on Jharna was more an issue of prestige rather than that of education and which in the future could be translated into an 'investment'.

Jharna always carried herself with élan and could easily be distinguished from other students of the college and its hostel. She knew well the 'ways' to maintain her singularity. Her every gesture proclaimed her financial status. It was obvious that where there is nectar, friends or rather the bees cannot be far away. By the time the first term of college ended, everyone had taken their 'place' around Jharna.

But even the thick mob of friends and unending flattery could not stop Jharna from noticing her classmate Jheel whom Jharna had been quietly observing for the last six months.

Jheel was charismatic and possessed an attractive personality. It was very clear that Jheel was mature and balanced. His characteristic courteousness and gentleness disseminated an aura which was hard to ignore. Jheel was not reserved but he also did not have a habit to confront. He mixed with people but never mingled with them. He could laugh heartily but as soon as he encountered even a hint of mockery or bitterness he retreated to his inner cave to isolate himself. It was public knowledge that the arrival of Jheel's bike in the parking lot meant it was time for the classes to start. He remained busy with his studies and simultaneously enjoyed the company of his friends. Unlike a hot sun easily felt, his presence like the soothing moonlight was subtle.

Jharna was keen to know Jheel better. She always had that strange feeling, while being among friends and acquaintances, of missing him. Jheel always greeted her with a 'hello' and just the hint of a smile on his face and would move on. There were times when this hurt her ego. One way or the other Jheel always hovered in her conscience. Jheel was so mild mannered that it was hard to be irritated with him. But it was equally true that he was hard to approach. His halo was like a drop of water which could drench you without your knowledge. Jharna wanted to get to know Jheel better. She began discussing academic topics with him, though she was hardly interested in the solutions he offered. She was more interested in him. Curiously enough, Jharna's presence never influenced Jheel and neither did her absence.

In the beginning the common topics that Jharna spoke about related to friends, films, cricket, food or clothes. Jheel did not seem to mind and listened intently. Sometimes he even grunted to affirm or jested in a few words but Jheel could not shrug off a feeling of inadequacy that she felt. Jharna always had that nagging feeling that she was near Jheel but never with him. Her desire to know and understand him had been growing. It was funny that approaching him was still a puzzle and yet it was hard to retract her footsteps.

Jharna's mind was often filled with vivid images of the two of them together. But these phantom thoughts never materialized and hours of futile contemplation never bore fruit.

There were times Jharna felt Jheel was testing her patience. Jharna had those occasional flashes that Jheel would never be able to understand her. Within these walls of silence Jharna was unable to comprehend the flavour of their relationship.

Jheel was sharp. He could guess the environment in which Jharna had grown up. Jharna on the other hand always wished that Jheel would ask about her family, her social and financial status but he never even broached the subject. He could sense what was going through Jharna's mind. Jharna would try to elicit information about him through an unending stream of questions but Jheel always replied in a terse 'yes' and 'no'.

Despite all this, slowly but surely a bond of friendship and faith was beginning to form between Jharna and Jheel. Jharna felt secure with Jheel. This nameless relationship had been there for some months now. Jheel had not cared to open the wrappers of the gifts which Jharna occasionally gifted him, though, he had also presented a few books to Jharna to reciprocate.

It was only a rare occasion that Jheel called Jharna. Today though unexpected, Jharna heard Jheels's voice as she lifted the receiver of the phone.

"Hi...Jharna! Would you like to join me this weekend?"

Jharna was taken aback by Jheel's proposal. After a stunned pause she asked -

"Jheel...is that you?

Are you sure that you are inviting me to come along this weekend?

Jheel...Jheel...Jheel!

I am really not sure that you are Jheel!"

Without any sign of excitement Jheel plainly said, "Yes Jharna, this is Jheel. Would you be able to make it?"

"Oh yes of course Jheel, I will...We will drive down in my car...Tell me if I have to get anything." Jharna could not stop chattering in her excitement.

"If you don't mind Jharna,we will go on my motorcycle. Also, there is no need to take anything along except your personal belongings," Jheel replied cuting the conversation short.

Jharna was euphoric. She would now have an opportunity to know him better, and best of all to be with him.

The winter was on its way out but summer had not quite arrived as that early morning, Jheel's bike made its way with Jharna clinging on to the pillion.

The rays of the rising sun laid out a golden carpet on the road for the young couple. It was probably the first time that Jharna was actually seeing the sunrise. Rising so early in the morning was not part of her routine. Jheel was a nature lover. He was completely immersed with nature while he rode the bike. Jharna was deep in her own thoughts. Somehow, she could not get herself to ask anything from Jheel. Occasionally Jheel would stop the bike and ask her if she would like some tea or refreshments and then the journey would start again. Jheel taking such good care of her at every step was a new experience for Jharna.

Jheel swerved his bike from the tar road onto a village path. They could see a range of hills from the rough and stony route. After riding for miles together on the rough road the bike seemed exhausted and refused to cover the gradient. They went uphill as much as they could. Jheel stopped at a spot and parked his bike under a tree.

"Jharna...C'mon... Now we have to walk up so you can sling your belongings on your shoulder...can you walk? You can give some of those bags to me."

"Jheel, where are we? Where are we going? I can't see any people here," Jharna said looking around.

"Jharna, I love to visit new places, to lose myself in nature. I aspire to meet people whose minds are as pure as the driven snow. These are the virgin Ratanmahal Hills in Panchmahals. I have heard a lot about these jungles, so I had to come here. Jharna... I do not have any intention to impose my hobbies on you.I only hope you do not get bored. And if at all that is the case, we shall return."

Jheel's words were reflecting his nature and behaviour, his voice revealing his feelings for Jharna.

"Hey Jheel... Is it okay for us to leave this bike here on its own? What if someone takes it away?" Jharna said in worried tone.

"Jharna, that urban disease is yet to reach these innocent tribal people. Don't worry, nothing will happen to the bike. These hills still remain unexplored, do you know that? There is a considerable population of bears here. This is a natural sanctuary of wild bears."

"Oh...God!"

There was fear in Jharna's voice.

"Bears..."

"Jharna, nothing to be frightened of...These tall trees which you see before you might be hundred and fifty years old. Possibly centuries ago there could have been tiny butterflies who may have sown them acting as nurserymen. Petrol fumes, urbanisation, tar roads, the glitter of the lights...The so called modernisation has not yet tainted this paradise."

"Jheel..It's really so beautiful. These houses are scattered so far apart...So far off."

Jharna was entering this new world for the first time. She was at a loss for words to express her feelings.

"Jharna...In the city we have established a farmhouse as a criterion for judging wealth. A sole house on a big piece of land maybe one, two or five acres of it. Just like a laboratory for getting counterfeit peace and happiness."

Saying this Jheel looked at Jharna to observe the changing expressions on her face. Jharna was blank. Jheel carried on the monologue further...

"Look at these scattered shanties made of bamboo, grass and leaves, these are the homes of the tribal people who live here.

Oh...Sorry! I mean these are their farmhouses. Dense woods...A distance of half a kilometre between two shanties...Just look at this

Jharna...The nature's bounties have come together... as if in blessing upon these happy and content lives. Moreover, Jharna these are not like farmhouses of the city people. These are real farmhouses. Shanties actually built from the farm produce. This is not a concrete jungle. No bricks, or lime or cement or steel...Nothing at all. This is a house made of the farm produce–bamboo, grass, trees, leaves..."

Jheel was engrossed in the praise of life in the forest.

For the first time Jharna felt that Jheel was in his true elements, expressing himself completely as if he had reached his favourite topic, among his favourite people, at his favourite location. It was a wonderful moment to know Jheel's true self. Jharna was feeling like a traveller who has just felt the first drop of water in his dry, parched throat.

One hill to another, one tree to another, they explored till the evening was upon them. Jheel and Jharna had come prepared to spend the night in the arms of nature. Jheel had inquired about the location of the village Sarpanch from a passing tribal. Both of them had hiked to reach a hut.

Jheel called out, "Is this the house of the village Sarpanch?"

A mature looking old man stepped out of the hut with cloth wrapped around his lower body and another cloth covering his head. He came out and greeted the couple with the traditional greeting 'Ram Ram'.

"Welcome...this is indeed Jodha Bhagat's house."

Seeing the guests, Jodha Bhagat shouted out towards the distant huts. In no time, there were five to seven elders from the village surrounding them.

Jodha Bhagat spread a couple of paper hoardings and some posters on the ground and offered the guests to take a seat. Jheel was observing keenly and could not resist asking with a tinge of amusement, "Sarpanch, these seem to be election posters. You have converted them into seats?"

Jodha Bhagat guffawed loudly.

"Young man, I doubt if the leaders in the city know us even remotely. They had sent about five hundred posters during the last election. How would they know that we tribals do not have walls around our houses in these woods, to stick the posters on? So we jolly well use them as seats." The sarcasm in his tone did not go unnoticed.

The amused Jodha Bhagat was laughing, seemingly over the politicians' poor grasp of the lives of his people.

As a simple supper was served to Jharna and Jheel, two youngsters swiftly climbed the nearby trees and began building a pair of 'machhans'. Within no time, there were two makeshift bedrooms for Jharna and Jheel ready to use in the middle of the canopy of the trees. Jharna was overwhelmed as she observed the happenings.

Jheel was addressing Jodha Bhagat as Sarpanch in the presence of other villagers. The villagers observed, "All of this is okay but that's Jodha Bhagat. Why don't you call him by his name?"

Jheel was taken aback and wondered : is Sarpanch not supposed to be an important post. Being a Sarpanch should surely be a matter of prestige and politically significant. People go to such lengths to become a Sarpanch. They should feel a sense of pride when addressed as Sarpanch instead of Jodha Bhagat. Jheel was curious and he asked a villager whose answer astonished both him and Jharna.

The villager said, "Sir, he has earned the epithet of a 'Bhagat' after due penance. He has earned it through the grace of God. Earned it after quitting all vices, by eating vegetarian food, which is rare in our society. 'Sarpanch' is just an administrative and political title whereas 'Bhagat' is a gift from God."

Jheel blurted, "Jharna...can you see this, can there be a bigger and better message for today's politicians?"

~

It was morning and Jodha Bhagat and his wife Jamna, Jheel and Jharna sat chatting under a tree just outside Bhagat's house. Jamna began talking to Jharna, lifting her head occasionally while she cleaned 'jowar' grains in a basket.

Curious to know more about them, Jharna began asking about the tribals' daily routine, their lifestyle and about how they make a living. She asked Jodha Bhagat, "I can see so many honeycombs in this jungle. Do many of you deal in honey?"

Jodha Bhagat gave a bewildered look to Jharna, but his face bore an expression of compassion as he answered, "My daughter, these combs are not for sale. We do not hold any right over them. It is a staple food of the bears who inhabit these jungles. What would the bears eat if we set up shops?"

Jamna interrupted, "Sinful even if we use a single drop of it...the honey."

Jharna glanced at the basket in Jamna's hands. Diligently she had separated the chaff from the grains. However, that was not all. She had divided grains in two parts. The small, somewhat wilted grain on one side; and the better ones, full and wholesome, on the other. Jharna was surprised to see that. She inquired about it. Jamna stared at Jharna. Looking down demurely, she explained "Both the jowars are to be milled, but the better grains are for making bread for Bhagat and these lesser ones are for me. I will make some bread for myself from these. Bhagat has to work so hard.

He needs to have the bread from the better ones. For me anything is okay."

Jamna's answer reached out deeply into Jharna's heart. Jamna's answer was enough for Jharna to experience goosebumps on her being. Jharna was just beginning to somewhat fathom the equations of a life of togetherness.

As Jheel dropped her back at her hostel Jharna was still captivated by the strains of the soulful melody of life which she had just experienced.

"Jheel, I shall ever be grateful to you for introducing me to, and letting me witness this life of love," saying this, Jharna ran towards her room, carrying with her the precious emotional bundle of her unforgettable experience.

Critique

Igniting Values : A parable on living a life of harmony and togetherness

Keshubhai Desai*

Our writers have insulated themselves from society, which has blunted their ability to communicate their message. Literature has always been a reflection of the society. It is common knowledge that collections such as 'Panchatantra'; 'Hitopadesha' and 'Jataka' stories are an exposition of moral principles or ideals which are usually told with the help of effective illustrations. Storytellers from the Gandhian era had employed the medium to propagate messages related to human welfare. Many of such works have remained relevant to this day. Chief Minister Mr. Narendra Modi was a person whose early exposure to the classics of Gujarati literature such as Dhumketu, R.V.Desai's stories or the literary pieces such as 'Rasdhaar' and poetry of Jhaverchand Meghani had moulded him into an idealistic young man. We have been getting occasional literary pieces from him in the form of poetry and stories under the infuence of novel philosophical principles of nationalism or self-dependent humanism. It has natural that while he dabbled in active politics and his duties as a pracharak[1] may not have allowed him to indulge in the 'riyaaz'[2] that a writer should undergo. He is more of an orator than a writer and more of a 'spoken language' person. Therefore, there is a fear that his works may have the tendency to be more conversational in style.

Inspite of these limitations, when an author writes stories, which are readable and gratifying, it is truly commendable. I do not know what are the opinions of seasoned readers about Mr. Narendra Modi's short story "Igniting Values" but personally, I got an impression that it shapes up well into a story that touches the heart. Certainly, it tends to exaggerate

* Gujarati novelist and columnist

idealism but the characters of Jheel and Jharna emerge as lively and idealistic lovers without being stereotyped. This is an achievement. The theme of the story juxtaposes two specific classes of society. On one hand, we have the life of a neo rich family believing in exhibitionism and on the other is the simple and basic lifestyle of the tribals. It is only natural that the sophistication and glamour of the life, which she is used to, are more important for the heroine Jharna. The author has attempted to enact the role of a promoter of an ideal society but at the same time has taken care not to dilute the characterization of the subjects involved. Through this, he has succeeded in creating amorous ripples in the heart of the young woman Jharna, who has tender feelings for Jheel. At the outset, even if Jheel tries to act aloof, unapproachable and indifferent ignoring the feeling of intense attraction; he has been watching her intently with a neutral eye from a safe distance.

He does not have an alternative but to bow before Jharna's irrepressible affection. He wishes to introduce her to his idealistic 'society'. To accomplish that, he takes her on a weekend expedition and they visit a remote location to get a first hand experience of the lives of the local tribals there. He gets an opportunity to let her hear all that he may have wished to tell her, through the mouths of the tribal couple. A girl brought up in a pseudo western setting habituated with all that comes along with an alien culture is enlightened after she beholds first hand, the culture of sacrifice and the power of mutual relationship. Then there is the incident when she receives an unexpected call from Jheel on her phone and Jharna was stunned for a moment. She could not imagine Jheel calling her. Even if she recognized his voice, she still confirms that it is indeed Jheel on the other end. Jheel has invited her for the weekend and thus begins a happy phase for Jharna. She seems as happy one would be on winning a lottery. She even offers to take her car along. The very idea of being with her flame is enough to bring on a wave of elation. However, the author's hero is as stable and sedate as Dhirodatt[3] and Dheerprashant, the heroes from the epics. He has already decided to go on his bike. Jharna consents. They start off on their trip to the Ratanmahal Hills of the Panchmahals.

Jharna would have preferred to go on a picnic. She represents the neo rich, modern, and materialistic youth. Nonetheless her co-traveller persuades her to accompany him to the unspoilt, pure location in the lap of nature where 'the minds of the men are as pure as the driven snow'. Jheel, who is so sedate and stable clarifies that it would be unfair of him to impose this idea upon Jharna and comes out with the disclaimer: "I only hope you do not get bored. And if at all that is the case, we shall return."

The author has created these characters conciously. His Jheel is the Maryada Purshottam Ram[4] of the 21st century who takes infinite care of Jharna while on the trip to the jungles. Perhaps she would have liked to spend her weekend in some fancy cottage. However, this was Jheel! He draws her towards the simple tribal peoples' hamlet in the hills for the 'equation of togetherness' lies there alone. The qualities of sacrifice and faith are rare among the city folks. This was truly an abode of love! Here Jheel emerges to be the real son of the soil draped in eternal Indianness, personifying the ancient culture of this country.

The highlights of the story are the dialogues. The author has always been dramatic in his oratory, which is evident in the dialogues of this story. It also reflects the poetic elements contained in his temperament. For example, "Jharna, that urban disease is yet to reach these innocent tribal people" and "Possibly centuries ago there could have been tiny butterflies who may have sown them acting as nurserymen."

The author gives a dramatic effect with Jheel's quotes. The simplicity, vitality and volatility of his writings call for an independent study. It contains the fragrance of Suresh Dalal's rhyme and Gunvant Shah's elegance. On the other hand the impressions of the reading he would have indulged in during school is evident in his writing, from the ornate structures and poetic design of the sentences. Like the poetic influence seen in Dhumketu's works, similar examples abound in his writings too. Another example is "Petrol fumes, urbanisation, tar roads, the glitter of the lights...The so called modernisation has not yet tainted this paradise."; Look at these scattered shanties made of bamboo, grass and leaves, these are the homes of the tribal people who live here. Oh...Sorry! I mean these are their farmhouses."

Jheel truly blooms in nature's lap. Actually, the author himself speaks through this medium. Both the characters seek out the Sarpanch's house in the tribal locality and stay overnight in the hamlet. Jodha Bhagat prefers to be identified as Bhagat rather than as a Sarpanch. A fellow villager clarifies that his real identity is not as a Sarpanch but Jodha Bhagat. All this because, Sarpanch is an administrative post, whereas 'Bhagat' is more of a bestowal by God.

The author himself is a well-known politician. His hero asks, "Jharna...can you see this, can there be a bigger and better message for today's politicians?"

The fundamental fact is about spreading the message. The author has not written this story for his personal satisfaction. He aims to give a specific message to the readers : The message of being Indian, and of the rapidly disappearing traditional ways of life. It is amply clear from such scenes as the way Jodha Bhagat welcomes complete strangers.

Perhaps, the posters on which they sat were the same ones sent by the political party workers (of Narendrabhai)! The tribals do not need to be educated about the ethics involved in using the resources made available by nature, limited to their own requirements.

Jodha Bhagat says, "My daughter, these combs are not for sale. We do not hold any right over them. It is a staple food of the bears, which inhabit these jungles. What would the bears eat if we set up shops?" Here even Jamna adds, "would be sinful even if we use a single drop of it...the honey." Of course, the author has in the course of telling this story, put forth a mesaage to protect the environment but the main element being discussed is still grihasthashram (the householder's duties)[5]. Jamna is an ideal homemaker. She makes bread (rotlas) for her husband. She keeps the better grains for her husband and the leftovers for herself. It seems that this particular episode shows the author going overboard. There are limits to idealistic thinking. Is it not a sin to keep the husband in the dark and keep the better grains for the husband while having the leftovers herself? Committing sati (figuratively) after the husband is clearly bourgeoisie ideology. While ruminating the past it seems that the author has forgotten the principle of equality for women. Sometimes, idealism from idealistic writers goes overboard in their over enthusiasm to give a message and may beget ridiculous situations. Even the fact about keeping the honeycombs for the bears may be hard to digest for the average reader.

Thus, this story turns out to be a "fantasy" more than a story - A parable. The author treats the characters like puppets and tries to put forth a message through this medium. However, an average reader and especially the teenagers may perhaps experience the thrill of visiting the jungles of the Ratanmahal Hills after reading this story.

Personally, I do like to read such tenderly written and yet inspiring works. Just like that jungle dweller, let me also wish the author: "Chief Ministership is a political and administrative post, but being an author is a gift from God." I guess we have a right to hope that the writer in Narendra Modi may blossom even more in the coming days.

---

1. Pracharaks are full time volunteers of RSS.
2. Riyaaz is an Urdu language term used for music practice, for honing of Hindustani classical music vocal as well as instrument skills.
3. Referring to the works of Jhaverchand Meghani.
4. Sri Ram is also known as Maryada Purushottam Ram because he is the epitome of righteousness.
5. Grihasthya refers to the second phase of an individual's life in the Hindu ashram system. It is often called 'the householder's life' revolving as it does round the duties of maintaining a household and leading a family-centred life.

Rebirth of Anuraag

Rebirth of Anuraag

One year had gone by. A year of great difficulty where each day, each moment seemed like an era.

The school building was the same.

The same old sports equipment.

Even the trees, leaves and the green surroundings remained the same.

There were the same old uniforms and just as before the same students and teachers.

The classes were conducted in the same manner with the teachers teaching from the same books.

The syllabi and the programmes too followed the same old routines, unchanged, except that everything now seemed lifeless and mechanical. It was as if life at school had lost its lustre. Even losing a loved one at home could have been forgotten with an effort less than this.

Today was the first anniversary of Amar's death. Amar's parents were going to the school, carrying sweet for the children in memory of Amar. As they entered the school gates they saw all the school-children standing around listlessly. They stood there as if it was an army of statues. Signs of deep sorrow and anguish were evident on each of their faces. Not a single hand was extended for the sweets that were being offered. The faces, each one of them, had the mark of guilt on them. The pain was noticeable. There was not a single pair of eyes ready to look directly into the eyes of Amar's parents.

It was as if a tormented darkness had descended at midday. None had the courage to accept the present. Each one was thinking of the event that had happened a year ago. The day Amar had died. The day Amar had attained immortality. Even a light rustle of the leaves or a whiff of air was enough to distract at that point of time. The air was hopelessly sad.

Piercing the pindrop silence like a streak of lightning suddenly there was a sound of loud sobs. The sound seemed to shake everyone upto their very core. It was after a full year that these sounds of sobbing were being heard for the first time - as if all the pent up emotions and feelings were finally finding their voice. It was not lost upon the students that the sound of the sobs was coming from their favourite teacher Anuraag.

It was as if Amar's death anniversary was turning into a day of Anuraag's rebirth. Anuraag 'Sir' was the soul of the school. Since the day Anuraag had joined school, the atmosphere of the school had seemed to bloom. It was as if the school walls, the large bell which tolled in between classes and even the plants in the garden had brightened up because of his mere presence. Whether it concerned the development of the students or their problems, Anuraag was always there. His just being there would fill the air with a purpose and any event he attended would take on the form of a celebration.

Anuraag 'Sir' was always on the go! The school and the students were his idea of bliss. Anything new that he would discover while reading or exploring were opportunities to inform and update his students. He worked hard so that his pupils were well informed. His excitement was infectious and he was the dominant subject in the students' conversations. Once he brought a television set during the Olympic Games so that the students could see the games being played "live". He regularly recorded the Games which could not be seen live and would later gather the interested students and show them the recordings. There were times when he came across some interesting Mexican food or pizza recipes while browsing a book and he would buy the ingredients himself and introduce his pupils to a new food, and making and eating it would become a fun-filled collective activity. There was never a book, which he read and did not discuss with the students. Also Anuraag never missed an opportunity to take the schoolchildren to the tents of a visiting circus or theatre troupe. He was a live fountain of boundless energy. Anuraag had sparked in his students an insatiable thirst for finding and discovering new facts and gaining more information.

But one ghastly episode devastated Anuraag's life. What remained now of his magnetic personality was no more than just a cage of bones and flesh. Anuraag seemed to be devoid of any energy and his speech buried deep down within and sunken eyes which never seemed to have the courage to look up.

Anuraag's active, benevolent and sensitive life was crushed between the wheels of pain arising from guilt. They say that one feels the intensity of feelings only when a sensitive life has completely been involved in another's. Ironically, his life had been devastated by his own enthusiasm and zeal.

Anuraag's loud sobs reminded everyone present there of the year old episode.

$\approx$

Exactly a year ago, a juggler with his performing dog had visited the town. As usual, Anuraag 'Sir' thought of it to be a good idea to bring the juggler to school. The juggler's dog was well trained and obeyed his master. The dog could recognize various denominations of currency notes. Upon instruction, he would unmistakably point out the student with a red or yellow kerchief. The dog was so trained that none who watched failed to be impressed. Then the juggler asked the dog to perform an unusual trick; he ordered the dog to point out the child who had thieved that morning. The dog walked by a bunch of students and suddenly stopped in front of Amar. That dog's stopping stated that Amar was a thief. The students giggled and clapped their hands at the dog's trick.

The show was over and everyone went back to their classes. There were a lot of appreciative whispers among the students regarding the skills of the dog. But Amar was feeling devastated and kept to himself. During the school recess the other students started teasing him - "Hey thief...Amar is a thief." And the calls of "Thief, thief..." became shriller and louder after school was over. Amar felt totally humiliated and did not know how to face this situation. All night long Amar could not sleep. The sounds of "thief!, thief!" kept ringing in his ears. No matter how hard he tried, he could not put the scene out of his mind. The next morning, he packed his books in his bag, touched the feet of his parents and set out for school. The trauma had taken its toll and Amar had made a decision. He reached a railway crossing near his school. It was only yesterday that a dog had conferred a certificate on him. Now he was waiting for a train to come and absolve him and certify his moral rectitude.

A train came hurtling down its way. Young Amar stood there without any fear. As soon as the train approached near he hurled aside his bagful of books and threw himself in front of the train. And suddenly...Amar was no more than pieces of flesh and bones!

Amar had bid adieu, but not without traumatizing Anuraag's life. Anuraag could never forgive himself. He drowned himself in feelings of penitence and remorse. He saw himself as the murderer of Amar. The juggler's dog had caused the death of Amar and it had been Anuraag's idea to call the juggler to school. Amar died a physical death but Anuraag had died from within.

Seeing Amar's parents in school, the numb Anuraag let himself go and sobbed for the first time since Amar's death. Amar's schoolmates also were reproachful. They seemed to realize their mistake and it was as if the gates to a deluge had been thrown open, sparked off by Anuraag's sobs. Amar's parents consoled Anuraag sincerely with open hearts. They tried their best to console the students too. Amar's mother built up her courage to say, "Amar is truly immortal."

Amar's parents could not save Amar but were determined to save Anuraag 'Sir', who had been dying every moment after Amar's death. The wailing Anuraag...was today demonstrating a will to live. The consoling words from Amar's parents brought comfort and on Amar's first death anniversary their sympathetic demeanour gave birth to a hope of Anurag's reincarnation.

A rebirth!

Reflections on the prevailing education system–'Rebirth of Anuraag'

*Priyakant Parikh**

Most Gujarati short story writers who are today between fifty and sixty years of age became popular authors when their stories were published in monthly magazines like *Chandani* and *Aaraam*. It is a pity that none of the Gujarati dailies including those from Saurashtra region and Maharshtra have any sub-publications in the form of a monthly magazine devoted to short stories.

First and foremost the identity of any creative person should be discussed solely for his creative ability and contribution; his or her achievements in the social, political, scientific or industrial fields should not overshadow him or her as a creator. It is extremely essential that this be taken into account and the work should be evaluated after due subtraction of other factors.

If we wish to enjoy the story 'Rebirth of Anuraag' from Narendra Modi's collection of short stories "Abode of Love" we ought to slice off the facts that he is an extraordinary orator with a sharpness that probably only Chanakya possessed, a Chief Minister who governs five crore Gujaratis and the conscience of the diaspora of Gujarat, and his multifarious personality. It is necessary that we should be reviewing only his skills as a storywriter, with which we shall proceed.

The stories from 'Abode of Love' were created and published long ago in *Chandani* and *Aaaraam* where 'Rebirth of Anuraag' was one such story, which represents a village school and conceptualizes an ideal setting of education.

In the introductory part of the story, the author has drawn a picture of pathos with the description of same old school building, the equipment

---

*   Eminent Gujarati novelist

for sports, the uniforms, textbooks and the teachers but all of them seemingly lifeless and lustreless.

What was the reason behind the pathos in a school perennially filled with joy and rapture?

The author has used the flashback effectively. The author draws us towards the reason with well-structured lines like "It was as if a tormented darkness had descended at midday. None had the courage to accept the present. Each one was thinking of the event that had happened a year ago."

This story is not a thriller; it is rather a purely instructive tale. Nevertheless, it evokes curiosity in the reader's mind.

The pindrop silence was interrupted by the sounds of sobs, which came like a streak of lightning. It shook most that were present there. It was after a full year that these sounds of sobbing were heard for the first time. The sound of the sobbing was an outcome of held up emotions and feelings since a year. "Where did the sound of the sobs come from?" sparks the curiosity.

The author is kind enough to feed the curiosity. 'It was not lost upon the students that the sound of the sobs was coming from their favourite teacher Anuraag.'

The author sets to build another path to curiosity. 'Amar's death anniversary had turned into a day Anuraag was born.'

Anuraag had been suffering from a feeling of guilt to such an extent that it had touched upon his personal life.

The author draws a detailed picture of Anuraag with just a few words.

'Anuraag 'Sir' was the soul of the school. Since the day Anuraag had joined school, the very atmosphere of the school had bloomed...'

Anuraag 'Sir' had boundless love for the children. He had brought a television so that the children could watch the Olympic Games. He made the students who were interested, watch the clips which he religiously recorded on tape. He made his pupils make and eat a variety of cuisines to extend their horizon. He took them to watch the circus. It depicted the interest he had in the overall development of the children. The children were his proxy existence.

Exactly a year ago, a juggler had visited the town. His job involved his dog from whom he elicited some fancy tricks...which included detecting the different coloured kerchiefs that the children carried with them. He even identified the denomination of currency notes. 'The juggler ordered the dog to point out the child who had thieved that morning' and thus began the climax of the story.

The dog stood before Amar (Anuraag is the hero here whereas

Amar is the alternate hero). Amar was labelled a thief by the dog. Other schoolchildren teased Amar. They called him "thief...thief". The delicate conscience of young Amar could not bear the humiliation.

Next morning, he packed his books in the bag, and started for school. The trauma had taken its toll and Amar made a decision. He reached a railway crossing near his school. It was only yesterday that a dog had conferred a certificate on him. He was waiting for a train, so that it may absolve him and certify his moral rectitude.

Anuraag drowned himself in feelings of penitence and remorse. He saw himself as a murderer of the child. Fellow schoolmates of Amar too were reproachful.

On the first death anniversary of Amar, his parents came to the school to distribute sweets. The atmosphere was sad.

The wise parents of Amar console Anuraag who is killing himself every moment of his life after Amar's demise. The parents attempt sincerely to convince Anuraag with an open heart. Amar's mother pays homage with just a few words, "Amar has really attained immortality."

Amar's mother's words act like the 'Sanjeevani' in Ramayan. They help dilute Anuraag's deeply embedded feelings of guilt. The words of sympathy touch Anuraag and bring him back. Back to a new life, a new birth. It was the reincarnation of Anuraag.

The end of the story became a beginning and so did the beginning an end. The beginning and the conclusion fused unto themselves, which speaks volumes of the author's skill.

The story begins in a simple and plain manner, somewhat in a Gandhian style. Notably, the language does not employ any English terms neither does it employ literary terms.

In these times, we need to have teachers like Anuraag whose mission is not just to impart knowledge but also ensure the overall development of their students. The world also needs to have pupils like Amar (not with reference to his suicide) and his parents who are wise enough to distinguish between the worst and best. This story is even more relevant in today's world rather than when it was written; with the burden carried by schoolchildren, and the overstuffed rickshaws plying them to and fro from school. In these times when education in one's own mother tongue is slowly and steadily becoming extinct.

Today, I am seeking a teacher like Anuraag.

I should thank Narendra Modi for giving us such a simple and straightforward story as "Rebirth of Anuraag". I only wish to have more such gems from his pen. May I cross my fingers?

Selected Quotes of Narendra Modi

◆

Each one of us has both; good and evil virtues. Those who decide to focus on the good ones succeed in life.

✳

Hard work never brings fatigue, it brings satisfaction.

✳

By getting an opportunity to serve society, we get a chance to repay our debt.

✳

Dreams are not seen when you sleep, dreams are those that don't let you sleep.

✳

The greatest quality that a person can possess is the quality of self-belief. If you believe you can, you can. If you believe you won't, you most certainly won't.

✳

Let work itself be the ambition.

✳

Each one of us has a natural instinct to rise, like a flame of the lamp. Let us nurture this instinct.

✳

Even small efforts to bring about a change in the social fabric eventually reap large fruits.

✳

Religion to me is devotion to work and devotedly working is being religious.

✳

Dreams must be steady (*sthir*). When dreams are steady, they take form of determination (*sankalp*) and when you combine them with hard-work, they turn into accomplishments (*siddhi*).

✳

No person is big or small. If we give emphasis on the dignity of an individual then change can be brought about.

✳

We should remain students for lifetime. You should be ready and yearn to learn from every moment of life. The basic elements of life need to be associated with learning. The learning process should be a part of your DNA.

✳

Reading becomes the fuel for development.

✳

No form, no manifestation of knowledge, is senseless.

*

Don't dream to be something but rather dream to do something great!

*

The root of democracy is in mass education. This foundation becomes stronger, when the citizens of tomorrow, our children are also educated about the electoral process.

*

I don't see dreams, I sow dreams! I try to sow a new dream everyday in the eyes of the people of Gujarat. If these dreams are realized, what else do I need.

❑ ❑ ❑